I0716690

NIGHT WORK

ADVANCED PRAISE

NIGHT WORK
by Pete Duval

"Part crime novel, part theological investigation, Pete Duval's brilliant and riveting **Night Work** reads like some lost Melville story, dug out of an attic trunk and updated for the seedy harbors of New England in the 1980s. Both a haunting and an act of grace, this is a novel of incredible power."
　　　　—**Mark Powell**, author of **The Late Rebellio**n

"**Night Work** is a speed-fueled fever dream of a novel, a breakneck thriller with the soul of a gothic ghost tale. Told in exuberant prose, it is a story that will haunt you long after you've read its final pages."
　　　　—**C. Matthew Smith**, author of **Twentymile**

"Pete Duval stretches reality like a rubber band. And never lets it break. **Night Work** is a fascinating work that finds a home somewhere between the mirages of Heart of Darkness and the illusions of Angel Heart. It's beautifully written, haunting, poetic, with all senses tingling. It's also an edge-of-your-seat thriller with a main character that taunts the reader with his closeness and yet remains a teasing 'other'. A strange book unlike anything current crime literature has to offer. A true gift."
　　　　—**M.E. Proctor**, author of **Love You Till Tuesday**

"**Night Work** is a contemplative thriller that leads the reader to the haunted edge along with its lead character Duchand. Pete Duval crafts an unrelenting story through a landscape of dark choices that will leave you with lingering ghosts."
　　　　—**Rob D. Smith**, author of **Good-looking Ugly**

PETE DUVAL

NIGHT WORK

2024

NIGHT WORK
Text copyright © 2024 Pete Duval

All rights reserved. This book or any portion thereof may not be reproduced or used in any manner whatsoever without the express written permission of the publisher except for the use of brief quotations in a book review.

This book is a work of fiction. Names, characters, places, and incidents either are products of the author's imagination or are used fictitiously. Any resemblance to actual persons, living or dead, events, or locales is entirely coincidental.

Published by **Shotgun Honey Books**

215 Loma Road
Charleston, WV 25314
www.ShotgunHoney.com

Cover by Bad Fido.

First Printing 2024.

ISBN-10: 1-956957-72-3
ISBN-13: 978-1-956957-72-3

9 8 7 6 5 4 3 2 1   24 23 22 21 20 19

*for Ashley, my wife,
and our daughter, Teddie,
and for my father, Ted Duval (1929-1992)*

NIGHT WORK

Be sure you make your home in this darkness.
—Anonymous, *The Cloud of Unknowing*

THE HOUSE OF THE DEAD

IT'S A GHOST HAND THAT SHAKES YOU, half real, and your body obeys, surfacing into consciousness. But then you're gasping and cold, the nerves in your neck stretched to breaking, your jeans clinging damp to you, and you scream, "João!" then listen to your breathing, raspy with phlegm, the only sound in a dark room, and there's the sharp stench of mold, and in the corner your sodden boots, one standing, one on its side, where you left them. If you let what you call your mind settle, this is what will come to you: that you know where you are. Alive and upstairs in the island cottage. The place they always called the windmill. Yet another unfinished ghost house from your past, ocean damp leaking in through the warped seams.

You drifted off, is all. Easeful sleep came over you, like warm oil. When you get your breathing under control, you might actually take account, your hand extended to the darkness as though possessed of its own eye, the better to know the gloom around you. What else are you sure of? That the pistol within arm's reach on the splintered floor is João's—or *was* João's. That it's an antique. (Was it ever fired?) Just like the antique nine-millimeter round you nodded off with under your tongue an hour ago. And with your tongue now you roll the bullet forward and back, careful not to swallow, though you're tempted to do so, ever on impulse, and a dream comes back, of choking on something metallic and unyielding and finally inside you. You click the bullet against your teeth. The salt sting lingers like the North Atlantic in your mouth.

How long have you been asleep?

"João," you whisper to the darkness. "Pray for me."

You roll onto your elbow to take the pistol, metal-chilled and heavy, in your eyeless palm, then settle back on your aching shoulder blades and eject the clip onto your stomach, surprised you remember all this— that you don't have to invent yourself muscle by muscle, string the sinews in your forearm or shoulder—then you spit the bullet like an olive pit into your other hand, snap it into position at the top of the clip, see the rounds receding with their tarnished copper heads, then feed the clip back into the handle and yank back on the slide. The pistol is loaded—all obedient and explosive potential—and this knowing floods you with equal parts satisfaction and dread. The same goes for the coiled rosaries nearby, the two sets intertwined, the blue-glass beads João gave you after your father died; and João's own set, of whale tooth, finger-stained with tobacco, yours now as well. No time to consider the logic of inheritance, though João was no relation, not through blood, at least. On the floor, in the low light, you do consider this cruel inventory, laid out to dry before you slept:

Yours, João's duffle.

Yours, João's vial of tiny white pills and his pocket-sized Order of the Mass, a color card of the Blessed Virgin Mary glued into its last pages.

Yours, a box of nine-millimeter rounds, its label in soggy Portuguese.

You ease the pistol's slide back into place and lay the weapon among these things. The power and the glory. But the one thing you really need—João's notebook, his "ledger," his illustrated history of his journey into the world of night work—this you do not have.

On your feet now, aware of a wooziness that could bring you right down again. Walking is a negotiation. The grit burns under your soles. Your mouth is salt-dry. Your skin is tight, your stomach blind and empty as a fist. You haven't eaten for days. And before that, just stale Wonder Bread and walnuts. At the window, you angle this way and that for a line of sight through the separated seams of the plywood, out onto the black waters of Buzzards Bay, the black waves like static that fades and rises. There's a rustling above you as of large birds struggling through crevices in the unfinished roof. Then, sudden as your waking, an upwelling of nausea bends you over, and you crouch, wavering and insubstantial, one hand on an exposed stud, until a series of dry heaves forces your voice again, clear and nonsensical in the silence. And you see João's eyes just after the last of the bales of weed had been taken aboard the *Padre Pio*. And you feel his hand on your shoulder, his casual touch like a rare language. And you remember his terrible grin—old world, all-knowing, and ashamed.

"João," you say to the cold room in a voice clear and frighteningly alone, "where did all that praying get you?" The truth of it enough to sear you. Like salt water in a wound but without the power to heal. The truth of it this: João is sinking into the North Atlantic, he'll always be sinking, he'll always be backlit, beatific, and all around him, in deep greens, the silence of the Mass. Like a father, a second father, gone like the first into that darkness.

You're going to need another of João's little white pills.

1

ON ITS COURSE back to New Bedford, the *Padre Pio* left a wake like blue frost between sea and stars. This, after a rendezvous in open water with the sorriest looking slum freighter you'd ever seen. You can still see it riding low-slung in the swells, its white hull streaked with dark rust and the look of absolute maritime dereliction. A vessel made for the night. The "mother ship," Kelly called it. Whenever he used the term in the days leading up to the trip, he'd lock eyes with João, like he knew what the old man was thinking. Maybe he did. Then João, attuned to the unfortunate, shameful implications of the phrase, would catch *your* eye, just for a moment. The veil would have parted briefly and João felt the sting of rebuke from the Blessed Virgin Mary herself, one of those cosmic "winks" João was always talking about, though anything but playful or comforting. Did Our Lady disapprove of night work? Any idiot could answer that. But then Our Lady didn't make a boat payment every month.

The handover had gone well. The seas had been calm. João had worked furiously, efficiently, for a man in his late sixties. He didn't have to. He owned the *Padre Pio*. He was the captain. But you saw it: he'd been fueled by nerves, sweating in the cold breeze right there beside you and Kelly and Mendoza, as you bucket-brigaded the lower cabins full, the head, the engine room, the kitchen, the kitchen cabinets, stacking as fast as they hurled the brown-taped bales from the freighter down onto the deck. João carried himself like a man both delivered and condemned.

But before he could give the order to start back for New Bedford, you watched a small man lower himself on the rope ladder as it slapped the hull of the mother ship. Rung by rung he came, his shadow, cast by the *Padre Pio*'s flood lamps, stretching and warping against the freighter's white and rust. The swells were building. The ladder swayed but the man managed the descent without effort. Kelly stepped forward to help him with the final yard or so. He took the man's hand and shook it, then led him over to João. And you thought, *son of a bitch*. You hadn't slept much, but there was no denying it was Berg. You don't know why you were so surprised. You'd heard the name. Berg was Kelly's contact on the other side, the reason any of this had been possible. But you hadn't made the connection. You knew Berg. You'd *known* him. He was local, a dropout at the Maritime Academy who'd faded from view and local public memory for two decades, to reappear, suddenly, as a "liaison" for the suppliers, setting up drops and coordinating new retailers up and down the east coast. Liaison. Right.

João said something brief but kept his hands occupied. He wanted nothing to do with the unsavory asshole. He was eager to start back. When he looked over, you saw something else—the hollowness and shame—in his face. Shit, you wanted nothing to do with Berg either. This wasn't your kind of people—or maybe you didn't have that luxury anymore. Maybe that was the real tragedy. You were crabbing along the gunnel heading below deck, but Berg spotted you. He performed a lame familiar little pantomime of shock, staggering sideways, with Kelly pointing at you and shaking his head. You couldn't hear what they were saying. You didn't want to. And Kelly laughed and waved you off. But then here came Berg himself. Goddamn it.

"Jesus Christ," he said, stepping among the drag chains, "I *thought* that was you."

"Is it me?"

He looked into your face with a strange, unnerving expression. "Never know who you'll meet in the middle of the goddamn North Atlantic." Then he laughed. "How's my favorite theologian? How's life, man? Good so far?"

"Hey," you said, "I wish we could chat—"

"Oh, come on, Duchand." He leaned forward as though to hug you, but your posture indicated such a gesture would be met with considerable reserve. His sneer brought a dead world back to life. Of rambling adolescent discussions on American foreign policy and medieval history and the improbable existence of God. The last had been Berg's favorite topic. You hadn't seen him since high school, a time of searing embarrassment made, in retrospect, somehow all the more so by Berg's relentless presence at your elbow. And how he knew things about you, you didn't want to think about. Things you'd offered in confidence because he'd been the only one who'd listen, sitting across from you in study hall, a scrawny guy, a scoffer with a weak chin and long stringy hair. All of these attributes still applied.

"This is rich indeed," Berg said. He looked back at Kelly for some reaction. "Ain't this rich?" He wasn't going to get one from you. "I'd have dressed better if I'd known." Then his narrow face lit up, his eyes shining. "Hey, Duchand, what do they call that, in Melville? You know what I mean? Oh, fuck. I can't think of the term."

Damned if you knew what he was talking about.

"A gam?" he said, eyes flashing above his broken eye teeth. "Yeah. Fuck me if we ain't in the middle of a goddamn gam! Just like in *Moby* fucking *Dick*. Shit! Duchand! Am I right?"

Kelly stood glaring from beyond. He wasn't warming to the idea that you had prior relations with his contact, the implications of which were too complicated to parse. He liked things uncomplicated. You wanted to uncomplicate them.

"You got any mail?" Berg asked.

"Any what?"

"Any mail," he said. "For the gam. Isn't that what they did? Exchange mail? Missives from motherfucking Nantucket, from the wives? Lonely on opium and tired of hiding their whale-bone dildos in the walls?"

You met his eyes without expression. "I think we're good, Berg."

"You haven't changed a bit, Duchand. Where's your sense of esprit de fucking corps? We're all in this together if I'm not mistaken."

A minute or two later, Berg had mercifully climbed the rope ladder and pulled it up after him, and then the freighter veered away from the *Padre Pio* and faded like a vessel made of mist. Kelly just watched you.

"What the fuck are you looking at?" he said.

Later, a little after midnight, well under way toward New Bedford, below decks, something shook you awake. The silence. No engine. You rose to pick your way along a tight path among the bales, checked the galley, the head, both crammed with gleaming packages of taped-up weed. The smell of fruit leaf mingling with salt and diesel and rust. No one. Nothing.

But then, out on the rear deck, there Kelly and Mendoza stood smoking, port and starboard, lost in their own worlds. Neither would meet your eyes. There was no moon, no wind. The stars seemed close and fat enough to choke on. Something wasn't right. A misalignment of the axes of being. You did a quick survey of the deck, of the remaining shiny bales stacked against the gunnels forward and back, of the wheelhouse above you, the Milky

Way glimmering through its windows. You mounted the first few rungs of the bridge ladder for an unobstructed view of the bow.

"Where's João?" you asked, lowering yourself.

Kelly's lips were moving, but there was nothing coming out. He seemed to be praying into the blackness beyond the reach of the flood lamps, but you knew him better than that.

Had they heard you?

"Kelly," you said, louder, "where's João?"

"Gone," he said, a little too quickly.

You laughed and looked over at Mendoza—who seemed deeply engaged in fiddling with the loose tape on one of the bales—then back. Kelly wasn't one to kid around. Even on legitimate fishing trips, which he still made, the man was all business. And ever since he'd set about arranging night work for João, he'd taken on a heightened air of menacing efficiency. He was married to your wife's cousin, but you'd never warmed to the man. Who could?

"Kelly," you said slowly, "what does 'gone' mean?"

"What do you think it means?" He was leaning on the far rail, just beyond the stowed dragger rig and the chaos of black rubber dampers. He tried to finesse one more pull from his joint, his Celtics t-shirt damp and filthy beneath his open mackinaw.

Gone over. João. Gone overboard. What the fuck were you supposed to say to something like that? Mendoza came up behind you, and you spun on him, dizzy. He had his hands out in those blue oversized work gloves he always wore, a strange and frightening expression on his unshaven face. You just stood there, glancing between him and Kelly, waiting for one of them to laugh and call you out as the gullible asshole you've always been.

"I'm not getting you," you said finally. "Mendoza, what's this asshole saying?"

Mendoza cocked his head with wide warning in his eyes. He was trembling.

Kelly smudged his roach in the rust, then pushed back from the rail to button his jacket. And there it was, lying by him on the uneven bales: the shotgun you'd seen him carry aboard back in New Bedford. João had seen it too; then he'd jerked his head for you to follow, and you had followed him, up to the wheelhouse, where, in the green glow of the radar, he'd tried to press the antique SIG Sauer P226 into your palm. *Are you fucking crazy?* You wouldn't raise your hands from your side. "Take it," João whispered, glancing past you to the deck. He was the captain, yes, but the rules didn't seem to apply anymore.

"Simple as that?" you asked Kelly now. "João's gone over? And you all cold as shit?"

"What do you want from me?" It was the way Kelly was trying to act, all nonchalant, that finally set your blood reeling. Trembling himself, unnerved, a new man, awake finally to what he was capable of, and failing to hide it from you and Mendoza. "What don't you understand?"

Mendoza was between you and Kelly now, mouthing, *No*, his eyes burning.

"So what do we do?" you asked. "What's the

procedure?" A stupid question. This was night work. There was no procedure. "Do we call the Coast Guard?"

Kelly grabbed the shotgun. "Mendoza, tell me this *retard* didn't just say what I think he said."

You backed away, feeling with your boot heel for the raised threshold of the hatchway.

"Back off, Kelly," Mendoza said, without much force. You could see him trying to find his own footing in the emergent order of things. In this new world. "João was like a father to him."

Kelly's face twisted with rage. "Fuck that sentimental shit."

You ducked into the hatch, two-stepped the stairs down to the galley. In the captain's quarters you dragged João's duffle from under his bed and fished around in it until you found the P226. You knew all about its seamy provenance: how it had been standard issue for the Estado Novo secret police back in the day. How João had come to possess it was another story, one he'd been less eager to talk about. How he'd known about these things, you'd never asked. But you had your theories.

Back in the galley, just as you sat down at the table, Mendoza rose up like a stencil in the door, sharp-edged against the milky stars. Could he come down, he asked, as though he needed your permission. You didn't say anything, but he ducked and came down anyway.

"Look, I know you're upset." His tone seemed all wrong, unpracticed, too cheerful. "But don't be an idiot."

You tried to discern his eyes in the darkness. His face wasn't his face. He'd been with the *Padre Pio* for years, since João had put together enough for a down payment on the dragger. Both of you had helped João scrape the hull, paint it robin's-egg blue, old school, and block-letter its new name in white. You can see the thing up on rusty stilts over in Fairhaven, João posing in the foreground for a Polaroid with his arm around Mendoza's shoulders, the two of them smiling and holding their beers aloft. Like coffee-skinned brothers—or more like father and son. Mendoza had that on you: he was of João's ancestry, Cape Verdean, his grandparents from the same island as João. But had Mendoza ever loved the man like you did? Had he understood the man like you? You, with your French-Canadian ancestry, and not a fisherman in the long line of unambitious dirt farmers and paste-white millwork-ers, and defrocked priests? But there was no jealousy for João's attention. You liked Mendoza. He'd been married for years, two or three kids, you forget. Clean ever since his wife had straightened him out. No drugs. He was a friend, of sorts. On the day you both heard João ask Kelly about night work, you'd been stunned, equally, in each other's eyes. Night work? This was João. "Most excellent," Kelly had said, like he'd been waiting all along for João's word. "I'll talk to Berg." It seemed to take just a day or two; Kelly had made all the arrangements, initiated con-tact with suppliers, set the coordinates for a meeting point with Berg's Colombian freighter making its way north from drops off New Jersey, cleared the transpor-tation logistics, rented the U-Hauls. It was a growing sideline for Kelly, a business endeavor well suited to his varied skill set. And though Mendoza hadn't said a word that day, you knew he carried it around like a wound. This was João you were talking about. João.

Now Mendoza leaned forward to whisper: "We have to play this right."

"We?" You felt around on the bench for the pistol. "Did you see it happen? Did you see him go over?"

"Use your head, Duchand."

Now you heard voices up on deck. Mendoza half turned to listen.

You stood up. "Who the fuck is he talking to up there?"

"Just don't go off, man. This is so unwise."

You pushed past him, climbed the stairs. Kelly was speaking with a man who, from behind, looked a lot like—

"What the fuck?" Was it Berg?

"See if you can hold it together for once," Mendoza said from below. He was trying, gently, to pull you back down into the galley. "He's from the mother ship."

"Yeah, I get it, Mendoza. Fuck the mothership."

You jerked free and swung up out of the hatch and climbed the bridge ladder to the wheelhouse and snapped on the flood lamps. The deck came alive beneath the harsh yellow light. Shielding his eyes, Kelly squinted into the glare, as the mystery man ducked and tightened his grip on what looked like a Kalashnikov. It was Berg, the son of a bitch, back on the *Padre Pio*. "Holy shit." Tentatively, as you came down the bridge ladder, to your surprise you were holding the Sig Sauer at waist-level. Was this you? Berg was on board, and João wasn't. Fuck it.

"All right, listen up," said Kelly, laying the shotgun gently down. "I can see you're upset. Let's take this slow."

"Isn't *that* a good idea." Berg's emaciated face was gray as dirty paste. His eyes sparkled. "You'd do well to calm down, Duchand."

"What the fuck is this, Kelly?"

"It's just Berg," he said innocently. "You want to put up the piece, you crazy fucker?"

Berg wore a bright blue watch cap pulled low over his forehead, and filthy jungle fatigues two sizes too big, and flimsy foam flip flops with white knee socks. Now he smiled through his broken teeth.

Kelly said, "Berg's raised a legitimate concern."

"About what?" you asked.

"The grandkid," said Berg, then lifted his eyebrows dubiously.

The *grandkid* was Antonio, whom João had raised as his own son, and who had sat in protective custody in the Ash Street Jail for weeks, in what many believed to be the capacity of material witness for the Bristol County DA. João had been driven to distraction and even tears— the first tears you'd ever seen from him—by the thought of his own flesh and blood behind bars. Not only that: everyone knew the kid would talk. It was a matter of time. Which was not something one did in New Bedford. All along Antonio had been making his own connections, dealing in the litter-strewn streets of the south and west ends, without João's knowledge and certainly without his consent, and he'd amassed an extensive and, in some estimations, valuable understanding of the distribution network, enough to do damage to the interests of not a few along the waterfront and maybe beyond. It was a situation that, together with João's wife's cancer and two missed balloon payments on the loan for the *Padre Pio*, had finally pushed João to night work. Otherwise João had been the cleanest man you knew, at least during his time on this side of the Atlantic. (You didn't know what to think about his days in Cape Verde, growing up near the Campo da Morte Lente.) He was the most devout man you'd ever met. But business was business, and he needed to score big, just once. In and out. One score. His wife didn't need to know, not that she was aware of much anymore. No one needed to know. Then he'd be done with it. And isn't that what they'd invented the Sacrament of Penance for?

"Look, I'll admit," said Berg, "it's unnerving." He turned to Kelly. "Aren't you a little unnerved?"

"I'm unnerved," said Kelly, smiling, "you could say that, yes."

"Are you unnerved, my friend?" Berg asked Mendoza. Mendoza didn't answer.

"Thing is," said Kelly, "they want to send a message."

"A message." You looked down. The pistol you were holding was aimed at Berg.

"Easy," Kelly said, his hand out now.

"Glory be," said Berg. He shook his head in mock amazement. "My favorite theologian has taken up arms. How things change. Or *have* they? Maybe it was always Praise The Lord and pass the ammunition."

"You can shut your mouth," you said.

Mendoza whispered from behind: "There's two of them."

"Yeah, I can see that," you said, leaning back. "Berg and Kelly."

"And another one," said Mendoza. "Be reasonable, man."

Kelly picked a shred of weed from his lips and spat daintily with the tip of his tongue. "Look, let's all just settle the fuck down." He edged forward, his hands raised in mock surrender. "Let's put away the weapon. This isn't like you at all. That's João's piece, right?"

"Where's your other man?" you asked.

"My other man?" Kelly turned to Berg. "Listen to this guy. It's plain to see he's unnerved."

"Put it away," said Berg. "You're just a bundle of nerves, my friend."

"Berg's showing some wisdom," said Kelly. "Show some yourself."

You yanked free of Mendoza again. "Fuck you, Kelly."

"Now, now." He took another step toward you, smiling big and fake. "Think this through. There's five U-Hauls waiting for us at South Terminal. We need to get back under way. You have no idea how embarrassing it's gonna be to come steaming in to New Bedford Harbor well past daylight loaded with—"

"Where's your other man?"

"OK, look. You're obviously retarded. So here's what I'm willing to do." Kelly stopped five feet from you, then craned forward. "Asshole," he whispered, hoarsely, "are you looking to get us *all* killed? Wise the fuck up."

"He's upset, Kelly," said Mendoza. "You don't get that? The man was like a father to him."

"No, I *do* get it." Kelly continued to glare at you with his wild eyes and that gray stubble that went up higher on his face than on anyone you'd ever known. He smelled of mothballs and singed hemp. "The man's unnerved. That's why I'm willing to take his outrageous behavior in stride, Mendoza."

"Where's your other man," you asked again, fighting the urge to point the pistol at his forehead.

Kelly turned to Berg and winked, and Berg shouldered his AK-47. "He wasn't like this when I knew him. Not that I remember. He was a reasonable individual back then. A self-proclaimed pacifist. So understanding. Mild, even. But not without his own peccadilloes. First and foremost of which was a timidness of soul. Where'd you get all this righteous indignation? What happened to live and let live?"

"Just dial it down a notch," Kelly said, turning back to you and Mendoza. "And we'll have a little pow-wow in the open out here. Put all our cards on the table and get ourselves under way. This shit is starting to chafe my ass."

Berg whistled into the night, yelled something in Spanish, and another guy in similarly ill-fitting fatigues and unfortunate footwear appeared on the bridge ladder opposite. He wore a Kalashnikov strapped to his back like an accessory from the fall fashion line, but he was also holding what looked like a rifle from one of the world wars. Another antique.

"Now Berg and his nice friend are going to relax astern while I climb up and see where exactly we might be," said Kelly. "Is that OK with you? And even if it isn't, would you do me small favor and stay put? Take a deep breath while you're at it."

Up close, you were suddenly aware of just how terrified Kelly himself was, every bit as terrified as you. This was a guy who'd scrapped with men twice his size, who'd kicked the shit out of a number of them, broken their teeth against the bar at the National Club, returned to his can of Narraganset without wiping their blood from his face.

"You can do what you want," you said, "but if you think I'm putting up my weapon, you're an idiot."

"Oh, Duchand, don't be that way," said Berg. "It's just bidness, my friend. The price we pay. I admire your caution, though, and I applaud your passion."

"One thing." Kelly set his foot on the bottom rung of the bridge ladder, his voice softening. "What's this about a ledger?"

"A what?" you asked.

"Good question," said Berg, sauntering closer. "A ledger is a little notebook you write shit in. To keep track of this and that. You never heard of one before? Really? A ledger?"

Mendoza leaned into you, his hand on your shoulder. You could feel him trembling, as though you were his shield against Kelly and these assholes with all the firepower. Maybe you were.

Kelly hadn't blinked in half an hour, it seemed. "Just the idea of it is raising some—anxiety. For Berg, and others. Understandably so. Even an idiot like you could see why."

"I have no clue what you're talking about." But you did. You had more than a clue.

Kelly smiled. "That's not what Mendoza told me."

"Fuck you, Kelly," said Mendoza, letting go of your shoulder.

"What have we become?" Berg cackled. "When we can't maintain confidences anymore."

"Mendoza," you said, nudging him. "I have to sit." He gave in and you both descended. You kept your eyes on the hatch all the way down, even while you sat at the galley table. There was a half-mug of coffee in a cup holder and you took a bitter swig and waited for one of them to appear in the hatchway. You pulled the slide of the pistol back slowly, felt the click, and checked the chamber. All set. Then you felt around in João's duffle for the box of shells, found it, laid it out on the table next to the greasy butter boat. You'd been wondering how one might keep awake for another six hours. Then, with a wash of relief, you found the vial of small white pills João always brought along but never seemed to take himself.

The seas were rising. The lamp rocked in its gimbal, its weak, watercolor-yellow light casting this way and that. You heard Kelly's boots above in the wheelhouse while Mendoza hunched over in the kitchen trying to light a cigarette. He was six or eight years younger than you, but standing there, he seemed like someone intertwined more inextricably with the sinews of this world than you'd ever be.

"I'm going to check it out," you whispered, and you crept back up the steps high enough to see Berg and his man sitting with their legs crossed at the ankles on arm-chairs they'd fashioned from bales of taped marijuana. Coming back down, you waved Mendoza over.

"Did you see it happen?"

"What?" But then he got it. He took a hit of his cigarette, red tip flaring and worming. "You think I could watch that?"

"I don't know, Mendoza, I'm learning a lot about the nature of things." Then, you almost didn't say it: "Could you?"

His grin. A flash. A skull's-head smile. That's how you knew you'd never make it.

Fishing in João's bag you found the rosaries—the one blue glass, the other creamy whale tooth, heirlooms from Cabo Verde, the old country that had hovered on the horizon of João's memory like a lost world, which it was—his Eden. And the miraculous medal, silver, black-creased from years of fingering, heavy as the coinage of antiquity.

For hours, making way back to New Bedford, the seas suddenly smooth with back-swell through Quicks Hole, then rolling again, you kept to your post at the table with its clear view of the hatchway, your shoulder blades flat up against the cold hull and the years of graffiti scratched in Portuguese and English. Mendoza had retreated to his room. Every hour you snuck to the top of the steps to watch the men out on deck—now they were lying with their hands behind their heads like careless campers—and you came back down and you waited, your eyes always on the hatch. You chewed coffee beans. When those ran out, you dry-swallowed another dose of João's speed and fingered the rosaries. You seemed to be rising—your head at least—into a new and different knowing. Your dark night, finally come, just as João had said it would. How it came to everyone. With this knowledge, your heart seemed to settle, because to die was what everyone did, but then your heart set to writhing again as though struggling through panicked crevices. No rest. Forget about sleep. Sometime during that long passage, your vision dancing with hallucinations, you made peace with all of it. And the tightness and the fear melted, and you had cruel leisure to look back coldly on the chain of days and disgrace that was your life. What wreckage. Your wife and daughters strangers to you. Your dishonorable discharge. Your forty-six years undone in a day and a night. But no matter. No matter. João said you had to be willing to throw it all away: here was your chance. That's what Jesus really came to tell us. Throw it away. Only then could you know true life. Eternal life? you'd asked. Forget eternal life, he'd said, shaking his head. Wasn't it enough to focus on this one? But if this be new life or true life or whatever kind of life, you were not impressed. Screw this shit, João. For real.

Mendoza lay snoring in his room. You kept the clip of the P226 in, the mechanism cocked, and ran your thumb again and again over the Portuguese coat of arms engraved on the grip. And just as you began to sink, Mendoza's voice seemed to reach down into that sweet darkness like grappling tongs and snag you by the neck:

Jump. Take your chances. Now or never.

He didn't have to say it again. You grabbed João's duffle and stumbled up the steps one last time and onto deck, which rang hollow under your boots, the pilot house lights still blaring, the salt air in your face. You stood gagging on all that surplus air, trying to get your bearings, to estimate where the *Padre Pio* might be. Not far from New Bedford, it turned out. Berg was asleep in a fetal ball. But his man stirred, sat up straight, flashed his eyes, and called out something in Spanish.

"Where do you think you're going?" Kelly asked, calmly, from above and behind you. Standing on the foredeck, leaning on the railing just outside the door to the wheelhouse, he held his shotgun as though coddling an infant.

You drifted toward the port-side gunnel. "What's it to you, asshole?"

"It's *nothing* to me." He shrugged. Then, almost conspiratorially: "What do you know about this ledger business?"

"Ledger?" You'd only seen it briefly. João had been keeping track of business, yes, writing down everything Antonio had ever told him, everything he'd ever seen. He was like that. He reveled in detail. Like some all-seeing eye. Book of life type-thing. Final witness. Insurance, you figured, against exactly the kind thing that had finally happened to him. A Cold War tactic gone wrong, a deterrent: mess with João you'd set loose terrible forces. Almost mythical in scope and feeling. And not just what he knew of Antonio's business. João wouldn't stop there. He'd go nuclear. What had started as a personal journal

decades ago had evolved into a goddamn illustrated history—complete with João's own drawings, watercolors,
diagrams—a guide to the waterfront in all its sleaze and
glory. He'd been part of the scene since time immemorial,
worked his way up from lowly lumper to crew member to
owner and captain. João knew some things.

"Kelly, what do you want me to say? I have no idea. You
seem to know more about it than me. What's a ledger?"

"Fuck you." Kelly wasn't as young as he'd once been
himself. But age—he was 55 or so—hadn't mellowed the
son of a bitch. He'd just keep hammering away as in days
of old. The wind messed with what graying hair stuck out
from beneath his wool cap: Boston Bruins logo facing
forward, black and yellow pompom limp with grease. He
was a big fan. He'd skated in a semi-pro league. At least
that's what he told people. One long night shucking scal-
lops, he'd spoken at length, and with considerable elo-
quence and rapt admiration, of Terry O'Reilly's mission
over the glass and into the stands of Madison Garden,
oddly gleaming as he described Mike Milbury's assault
on a Rangers fan with the man's own shoe.

"I can't figure you out, Duchand," he said. "You think
you're not implicated in all of this? You think your shit
don't smell?"

The stranger had risen to his feet. He nudged Berg
with the butt of his rifle. Berg snapped awake and immediately broke out with cackling glee. "Say, now," he said.
"What's happening?"

"Everything's just fine," said Kelly. "Go back to sleep."

"And miss the fun?"

"Think of João," you said to Kelly. "This is João we're talking about."

"Nothing's going to bring the man back."

The black crags of Angelica Rock and Wilburs Point beyond were parallaxing off the starboard side. Your brain seemed jammed with ice, but you estimated the distance from your position there in the entrance channel to the tip of Black Rock, just off the point, at five hundred yards. You edged toward one of the outriggers, its stabilizer swinging slightly in the wind above you, and worked your arms through the loops of João's duffle, into which you'd shoved an orange net float.

Kelly paused half-way down the bridge ladder.

"Oh, fuck me," he said, realizing what you were up to. "You're more retarded than I ever imagined. Where's Mendoza? Mendoza! Look at this self-destructive fuck. You gotta see this."

Mendoza crouched at the top of the cabin steps, just inside the hatch, beyond the reach of the flood lights. He hadn't warned you for nothing. One of those U-Hauls waiting at South Terminal docks? It was reserved for your corpse to ride along with the weed. If you even made it that far. You strained to see him in the darkness there: he was mouthing, almost angrily, the word *Go, go!* He seemed to have found a weapon of his own, which might have been the goddamn flare gun.

Kelly spat into a mound of line below him and scratched his head with the shotgun's muzzle.

"What are you going to do, Kelly?" you said, stepping

up onto the outer rail. It was only about four inches wide. "You going to kill another crew member?"

Kelly grinned mercilessly.

"So dramatic," Berg called across the deck. "Kelly, is he always this dramatic?"

The outrigger jangled as you mounted it. You worried it might give way, swing you down to shatter your body against the hull. You climbed anyway.

Kelly finally leveled the shotgun at you. "Don't make me waste your pathetic ass."

Berg whistled. "Is that necessary, Kelly?" He tapped his man on the shoulder and he started for you.

But you kicked free to fall clear of the hull.

"Is it always like a fucking opera with you guys?" you thought you heard Berg say.

The water burned cold as it swallowed you, forced itself into your ears, stopped them up. In the near darkness the props churned and flashed like butcher blades. You thrashed out, clawing, unsure of up or down, trying not to gasp. The cosmic thrum of the engine shook your rib cage like the voice of God.

You surfaced, sputtering and bobbing in the black chops. But the float in João's duffle forced you face forward as you fought and gasped and flailed, until you managed to calm your panic long enough to pull your arms free and clutch the bulk of it to your chest. You heard gunshots, but they seemed far away now. Then voices from the deck. Then something like keening laughter. Berg's falsetto laughter. The *Padre Pio* seemed to turn to starboard, but never slowed, thin as paper against the lights of New Bedford, moving on toward Butler Flats Light and the harbor entrance in the hurricane dike a mile away. There was no time to watch it go.

Miracles. João had spoken of them. Reckon these: That the complex currents of Buzzard's Bay pushed you eastward rather than south or west toward open water. That you'd leaped at the most fortuitous possible moment, just beyond the outstretched hand of Black Rock, its granite outcrop, and the unfinished house built to look like a windmill without blades. Your unfinished windmill. That in the moment your legs began to cramp, a green channel buoy offered itself up that you might rest, clinging to it, and moan with the cold.

A loneliness so deep out there, to wring the last of what's human from you, to suck the voice from your lungs and mind, and leave you kin to the legions of the drowned.

"João!" you called out through stiff lips. You weren't entirely sure if you could speak or not—*Pray for me!*—as you shoved off to thrash the final 300 yards, shrieking with each breath, gagging into the chops that slapped at your face. *Pray for me, João!*

Then, incongruously, you were scrabbling in the salt wash, striking out with your boots for purchase among the barnacles and mussels, your hands burning but numb, stiff, useless. You scaled a rock face slick with bird shit, to where the granite leveled out and you could crouch in the lee of the windmill house, warm your fingers in your armpits, delineate your heaving ribs, reconstruct your sense of space and time. The universe reeled, and rocking to its cadence you counted to 15 before forcing yourself to stand up against the November wind. Then you circled the dark house to pry the plywood from one of its southward window wells.

You know this place—Klein's windmill—because you built it. You'd just begun finishing it out—one of your many jobs, odd or otherwise—when Klein's final appeal for a variance was rejected and he and his inexplicably cheerful trophy wife—a woman whose interior glowed like coals behind frosted glass (you'd never seen into Klein himself)—came round at high tide in a dinghy to deliver the news in person. He was such a stand-up guy. "Missed it by less than a foot," he'd said, smiling the smile of a man who'd get something for his money, if only the joy of ruefulness. He could afford it. No building on that rock, no exceptions, even for structures on stilts or supports, there simply wasn't enough of it left above highest tide. Which you'd known. But all along he'd talked right over your objections. This was why no one had built here before, you'd told him, with the outcrop's gorgeous views of the south-facing bluffs of Naushon Island and, on a cloudless day, all the way to Cutty Hunk. Didn't you tell him he'd get nowhere in this town? One had to know someone. Klein was from Boston. All he'd had was money. Mega bucks. Standing in the dinghy with his wife all aglow from within, he'd laughed. You hadn't seen into anyone in a long time, and you were having difficulty concentrating on the conversation. *Fuck these hicks*, Klein had said. He'd build again, on the North Shore—had started. Said he was voting Republican for fucking sure next time, as he peeled off a few hundred-notes for your trouble.

Inside, now, you scrounged the cellar crawlspace, then the attic, found a kerosene heater with a trace of fuel in it and some floor space on which to arrange your clothes in a semi-circle to dry while it burned down to blackness. Your hands burned salt-raw and reeked of rust and machine oil and bird shit. Your blue rubber boots stood by the room's unattached door, one standing, one on its side—the boots of a dead man—and the hollow sound of wind through the eaves and plywood. The house would return to the elements some day. You crouched on your heels again in the fading circle of meager heat, wondering why you even bothered to fight sleep.

João never pushed it on you, those darker edges of his knowledge. Not too hard, he didn't. He had a box for anything you could bring: hypotheticals about aggressive and incurable cancers, which in time had become quite un-hypothetical; serial killers; the death of children at the teeth of German Shepherds—bring it in any guise and call it what you want, it didn't matter. João knew from whence it all originated and how faith, if it meant anything, had to prevail in the face of the worst of it. Faith in what? "You live in this world," he often said. "This one. Not some dream world." And this world was more than good enough. It was God's body. On his last night, beneath decks, you watched him change his shirt, a thin man on the doorstep of utter old age. He lifted the scapular to show you, again. You'd seen it before. He wore it draped over his wiry torso, front and back, two sweat-stained swatches of green and brown cloth tied with what looked like flat brown shoe string. So simple. He drew comfort from Our Lady's promise against hellfire. You'd heard it all before. Our Lady of Fatima was not one to mess with. "I'm the first to say, I hope you're right," you'd said. But you never told him about what you yourself had seen. He never opened up in that way. Never glowed for you.

Standing here, now, fully awake in this house of the dead, your feet cold as dead men's feet, you don't even have to close your eyes to see João's scapular curling in slow motion down there in lightless currents, the swatches still clinging to João's neck, the spectacle of it all burgeoning at first in the green-lit chamber of your imagination, then emerging slowly into this forgotten room, not five feet from you. Fading and flickering, there and not there. Kin to the inner glow that some manifest to you (though you can never predict who will, who won't—you've given up trying). It has been years since you saw your father, in the months after his death; he was sitting cross-legged on your kitchen floor, his head down. So long now, you have to fight the urge to ask João, there among the newly dead, for word of him. But even the dead can sniff out indignity. Maybe more so than the living. Are you sure he has no advice to share, no news? The living make their own way. "What about it over there?" you ask the darkness, finally. You have no shame. "Anything to report?"

No. Not a word. The dead no more articulate than the quick.

Enough. You dry swallow another João's white pills. Forget the dead. You're alive, for now—the words *more so than ever* flash in your speed-juked mind—and aware that something very real is required of you. You need to take stock. You need to take a look around. To get in touch with the here and now. "*This* world." To see what is, that is wisdom. Gather up what tools present themselves. There are always such tool at hand. You feel the service pistol. It seems to reemerge into being, though you've been holding it all along. You eject the clip, check to see if it's still full of heartbreakers, still fully loaded—it is—snap it back into the handle. It feels good to be sure. You hang the rosaries, both sets, around your neck. There'll be time enough for sleep.

Give my best to my father, you want to tell him, but João is all impenetrable smile again, all pallid and joyless, as if to say, *You know better, my friend, haven't you learned a thing, you're almost an old man, it doesn't work like that, it never did.*

<h1 style="text-align:center">2</h1>

OUT IN THE RAW AIR again, you strip naked and stuff your stiff-dry jeans into João's duffle with the orange net float. The tide is receding. The water coils, swelling among the rocks thickly, smooth as black glass. You manage the slope of the granite outcrop in your sockless boots, then wade a hundred yards waist-deep toward Wilburs Point, gliding in the November darkness, your feet crunching ocean litter, João's duffle over your head. It's open water. Your thighs grow numb again. Like the rest of you. They are you and not you.

Dark against the lightening east, the Point's outermost cottage crouches on stilts over its garage. Barefoot, you cross three brittle yellow lawns set off by low stone walls and dead sea rose and thistle. Behind the garage, you dress, your clothes like death as you pull them on. You break out a window in the rear of the building with the meat of your fist, weasel through, drop hand-first onto a workbench, the rosary beads hanging below you, knock over a coffee can with pant brushes and turpentine. There. Shrink-wrapped in glossy white plastic, you find it: the Jaguar—or the shape of one. It belongs to Klein's former summer neighbors, a pale and ancient couple from old Newport. You remember the husband's two last names and condescending eyes, bright and cold, the smile that spoke of his confidence in dealing with the rougher class. It's the "summer car" you once contracted to start for the man and to allow to idle twice monthly during the winter season. You stood at the end of the driveway while Klein vouched for your character and only then called you over.

The smell of turpentine to sicken your stomach. You find a box cutter hanging from a peg board, slice away the shrink-wrap, which separates like drawing open a zipper—clean and efficient—to reveal the car, an antique model, the 12-cylinder coupe. You find the keys among the shards of a blue milk bottle. When you crack the door, there's a blast of must and mold as you lower yourself into the cold-crackling leather seat. The perfume of automotive mausoleums. The engine coughs—you have to pump the gas, take care not to flood it—but finally turns over. The miracles keep coming. The resurrections. You get out to lift the garage door to the magic hour. And you're wavering with fatigue and hunger as you stand there looking at the car in the predawn light and feel the edges of a blooming loss of nerve. You're not a confident thief. There's not much gas in the tank. You don't need much to get to João's apartment.

You haven't been there in months, though at one time you played chess weekly at his kitchen table. After his wife fell ill, the air seemed laden with a sadness too sodden to breathe, which shames you now when you think of all that João did for you and your mother in the months after your father's death, and for you after your mother's. But there was the topic of the Church, your slow spiraling away from it. From the sacraments. From what you came to see as the senseless, empty, joyless ritual. The result was a nothingness that lingered unremarked in the air of João's kitchen. What could you say? Not that João ever pushed anything on you. Those discussions, when they happened, were always your choice. They kept you coming back for a while. You never could resist fingering a wound.

No one else on the roads but a Nissan bread delivery truck stinking of diesel. As you cross the green bridge into New Bedford, you crane to see beyond the guardrails whether the *Padre Pio* is still tied up at the South Terminal pier. The lights of the harbor markers glow cherry red, as dawn opens up like a blue smear now. All of it yours and not yours. As though you're dead already and free to roam at will, the sooner to drift beyond the limits of the corporeal. You debate whether to dry-swallow another amphetamine, because your chest is already light as air, your mind squirreling, nimble. Like snow on a broad brown leaf, ready to slide away.

The South End. João lived on the second floor of the duplex he owned, the narrow hall smelling always of oranges and homemade cleaning supplies. His door key loose in the duffle, you leave the Jaguar on a parallel street, lope along the driveway, scale a shadow-box fence, aware of your age as you drop into the frosted grass of João's winter lawn. Cinder block garages all around, with dark hip roofs and green-stained walls. New Bedford of the 1930s lingering still. T-shirts and enormous yellow house dresses billow from bowed lines.

Inside João's apartment—the order and the cleanliness. The sense of the man's presence still. This man. The driftwood crucifixes and hand-strung rosaries hung from nails in the walls. The unsent postcards and faded prints of Jesus as a young Cape Verdean, his dark skin radiant. A neat stack of weekly bulletins from Holy Family Church. Our Lady everywhere, her blue robes, her smile, her secret knowledge—of everything, down to the hour of your death. *Pray for me.* Dishes in a homemade dish rack. An easel in a side room without window curtains. João's home-stretched canvases stacked against the one bare wall. He was a clever man. It revisits you, the airiness of your mission. The way your heart crabs and sidles in your ribcage. No time, no time. Though one portrait looks familiar: head and shoulders in a scary profile against the red bricks of some abandoned cotton mill. Half-sketched, unfinished. Is it you?

Focus. The ledger.

The silence urges you on like crowd noise. You go through the obvious places. You're into dresser drawers, under the mattress, under the bed. You're trying to think like João but realize more and more it's not easy. You're up on a step ladder, fighting the anxiety you might fall to the floor for your lightheadedness, groping along coarse pine shelves in the back of a narrow closet, confronting the dailiness of João's smell. It's heady. The earthy stink of panic now. Knowing you won't find the ledger where you'd expect, you try not to expect, but it's difficult to look because to look is to expect, to find. But there's no other choice. The ledger is the ticket. But where to? Away from here. On the death train. And you hear the loop in your mind finally.

You descend the step ladder and turn to confront João himself standing not five feet from you with his brown sinewy arms crossed. Ignore it. It's just the speed. It's the sleeplessness come to life. He's intermittently vivid, there but not there, irreducible, shadow-casting João.

"Oh, shit," you whisper. "Here we go."

At the touch of your voice, his outline shimmies, burns, readjusts, merges with what's behind him. Like your focus. As insubstantial as forgotten thoughts. He is the way—your reasoning faulty as ever—we look to ourselves in dreams. Is he there? The confrontation—its logic—rouses your slumbering skepticism about the stories from his youth, how he "saw" the Blessed Mother from the uneven rooftops of his impoverished neighborhood in the Cape Verde. Island of Santiago. Because what is "seeing"? And do you have time for this shit? No. An eight-year-old kid at the center of the growing fanfare, the visits from agents of the Holy See, and crowds of pilgrims from neighboring islands, the grinding monotony of island life lifting, finally. But she faded as he grew older, then completely disappeared. It took him years to "let her go," as he put it. But João was always too eloquent in his descriptions of her for your tastes, as though he'd only read about it somewhere. A storyteller's appetite.

"You've got much more pressing problems right now," he says, his voice strained, seeming to issue from beneath crushing weight. You fold the step ladder as the old man glimmers and shape-shifts, all the while you're debating whether to address him and make a fool of yourself, if only to yourself. What is seeing? Already you're looking past him.

"What about your family?" he asks. "Have you given any thought to their safety?" He doesn't mention your wife or two daughters. Not by name. And at first you wonder if he's talking about your parents. Over there.

"If you think I'm going to carry on a conversation with a dead man, you're morbidly mistaken."

"The ledger," says João. With difficulty, he draws a long, wheezing breath, then scratches an unshaven jowl in an attempt at slightly distracted old-world masculine nonchalance. Dead or alive, you know this man. "Yes," he says, "exactly. In the attic, accessible above the outer hallway, over the landing." His clothes—*vestments* is a better word but one you resist for reasons obvious—seem to blossom around him. "The Lord is not what you'd think."

"Right." You hurry past him with the step ladder to the landing. Might as well take him up on it. No good suggestion turned aside. If you keep busy, he'll fade. But you can't resist. "And what would that be?"

Sheepishly, João follows you to the doorway. "It's colder here."

"Where?" you ask, regretting it. You're aware of your heart thrumming in your temples, your empty chest. Because there's nothing else in there. "You're in no place."

"Visit her," João says. "It's very important." He's trying to disguise his own troubled breathing. "For a number of reasons."

You're on your toes at the top step of the ladder. You know who he's talking about, which makes sense—how could it be any other way?—because he *is* you. A dream. A projection. Annoyed, you pause in your fumbling with the trap door above your head. "Why me?" This question makes no sense. You make no sense.

João just watches you work, his chest heaving.

You thrust finally up into the attic, engage the warmer layers of static air, slide the plywood away into the dark.

"And Antonio. He has something for you."

"Hey, why not just visit him yourself." You don't like the way you sound— constipated, whiny. "For Christ's sake," you whisper. "It's not like you have anything else going on."

Wait. Hold still. Someone's at the outer door downstairs. They're not bothering to knock. Your hand raised, you hush him. You hear them bluster in like they own the place.

"Any idea who that might be?" you ask, though you know damn well who it is.

João looks worried but manages one of his pained smiles. The expression has begun to annoy you. He says, "You have a *number* of misconceptions about the dead."

"But no illusions, believe me." You struggle to pull yourself up by your aching elbows into the attic.

"Where's the sidearm?" João asks up after you.

"In the car."

He nods, thoughtfully. "Perfect."

Footfalls in the first-floor entryway. Pounding on the door of the lower apartment. Antonio's apartment. He's not there, he's in jail. You hope his girlfriend isn't home. You motion for João to hand you the step ladder, but the old man just shakes his head as though ashamed. So you grope around, knock over a flashlight standing on end at the edge of the opening, then palm a curtain rod in the dark, draw it free, lean forward, hook it into then ladder's flanged platform, struggle to lift it into the hole after you, do so, miraculously, then thrust it away to secure the rough-edged rectangle of wood into the hole just before boot steps on the stairs reach the top landing.

Voices below. Hoarse, staccato. This is real. The terror catches up with you, surges into your jugulars. Your head begins to swim, your perception troubled by waves of dread, an excitement in your chest—turbocharging the effect of João's amphetamines, which seems ready to explode into exuberant, involuntary song, but you settle into it. You regain control of your breath.

It sounds like Berg down there, of course. He's shrill as ever, all falsetto, and unnerving as hell. There's someone else with him whose voice you don't recognize. You scrape along the boards on your elbows and ankles to a spot roughly above them, press your ear to the gritty floor. They're tipping things over, dragging things down, behaving exactly the way men trashing a place in search of something they're afraid they won't find are supposed to behave. Now they're breaking glass. Now they're hammering holes into the walls. Swearing with hateful glee as they do so. It worries you just how shrill Berg sounds. It's unearthly, almost comical. Their boots on the landing again, their voices clearer now. Another fucking miracle, how they don't simply raise their eyes to the trap door above them. Growling, scuffling. Berg's falsetto laughter. He's a cartoon. Now they're descending in a rush past the screams of João's first-floor tenant, Antonio's girlfriend.

You scrape and rise—there's not much room overhead—snap on the flashlight you found at the edge of the trap door. More furniture, all of it covered in translucent sheeting. Things you'd see in a sacristy. Or a Catholic supply store. Floor-standing candle holders. Brass monstrances wrapped in dusty plastic and masking tape. Censers hung from the central beam. More images of the Blessed Virgin Mary than you could count. You watch her eyes, daring her to blink in the glare of the flashlight. Beneath a round, rose-colored window leaking dawn, a low wide chest of drawers, which you get busy opening one after another. It's not easy; the wood has swollen tight. These are furnishings from another century. You crouch, breathe, start again, pushing aside the wells of religious gimcrack, stirring and fishing, knocking for false drawer bottoms, then fine one.

Open it. There is it. The ledger. Easy.

"That's not it," comes a voice from behind you.

You open the book anyway. It's blank.

"Here." With a pained release of breath João crouches in the far corner of the attic, beneath a slant of bare rafters. He points to the floor under what looks like a cherry wood confessional or maybe it's just the papal wardrobe.

"A simple please would be nice."

"Slide it over a foot or so," he says, tapping the thing. "That's all you will need."

"How the hell did you get that up here?"

You struggle against the mighty thing, rocking it, raising dust with your boots, scraping its claw-handled legs along the soft pine of the floor.

"Did you know," he says, pausing for breath, "that there are secondary meanings for the word *ledger*?"

"Fascinating, João. No, I mean it. Fill me with wonder."

"See?" He shifts on his ghost haunches. You can smell what passes for his breath, an essence of clove cigarettes and Turkish coffee. Of mothballs and decay. "There's a panel."

Yes. Finally. You find it—them, ten, twelves volumes— nesting in a filthy cloud of ancient insulation. You lift one volume out. An urgency snakes into your ribs. The ledger. With each throb of your heart you seem closer to passing out. For a moment, your vision narrows. The ledger. Yes. It's your ticket. You're dead with it, but you're dead without it, you and—

Like a bellows, João draws a stringy breath. "The word

can also refer to a rectangular cut of stone laid out flat over a grave."

"Don't mind me." You open the book. "I'm just trying to save my life." Pages and pages of longhand. Illustrations with crosshatch shading of people you recognize, though most you don't. Drawings of buildings from, you guess, Cape Verde, ruins, ivy-cloaked and sun-drenched. It's all done with a fountain pen, the drawings and the text, in a neat miniature hand that gets darker as you move further in. You pick up another volume—the same, though the ink has faded to sky blue. "How far do they go back?"

"Far," he says.

"*How far*, João!"

As an answer, João points to the first volume, which you lift from the swaddle of pink insulation. The handwriting is in pencil, in what you take to be Portuguese, a child's scratch that struggles to follow the hand-ruled lines, but most of it's drawings, and watercolors that have warped the old paper, of the same face over and over again. As you flip through the pages, the illustrations become more assured, shaded, the penmanship steadier. You look up. João is staring at the floorboards.

"Take them," he says. "All of them."

"This is what the fuss is all about? This?"

"No," he says, "there," pointing at the last volume. You crack it open, fan through the pages, notice immediately that at some point the writing goes from Portuguese to another language, which you've never seen before. There are dates, sums, maps, timelines, but the writing after that point is indecipherable.

"My own private notation," he says, smiling, proud. "Do you understand?"

"No, I do not understand, João," you say. "That's what makes it private. What the hell do I do with this?"

"You will need the legend."

"The legend?" You turn to look squarely at him. This close, his corporeality proves to have been deceptive. He's not all there. "Can't you just tell me? Save me some time?"

"The legend," he says, smiling wanly now, as though he's enjoying this. "So you can read the ledger."

"The legend for the ledger, João? Are you serious?" You flip through the pages once more, quickly. "Am I mentioned in this thing?" For a confused moment, you're looking for your own face among the drawings and writing, and you're disappointed not to find it. But do you ask? No!

"See her," he says, sad now.

You already know who he's talking about, his wife, Agostinha. She has cancer. There's no hope. There never was, right from the beginning. None. She's in hospice. You know where. The West End. A bad neighborhood. João hadn't talked much about her. She was just always there, not exactly in the background. You know her as a patient woman. Long suffering and archetypal. From the old country. The lineage of mystery, leading back you don't know where. Absolutely on anyone's short list for sainthood—anyone who'd bother. You and she may have exchanged fifty words of conversation in all your years. Not that you didn't try, at first. Then she wasn't there anymore.

You smell wood smoke. You smell singed electrical wiring. Sharp and bitter. It opens up a door through your memory into a lost world, into a space bounded by feeling. You hear a scream. You hear the shattering of windows. Close up now, João meets your eyes, frowns just as you realize what's happening; it's like he's wired into your addled mind. The bastards have set fire to the apartment below, which is only now blossoming into conflagration. You stand up, slam your head against a rafter.

"Son of a bitch."

"In the base of the crucifix," João wheezes, still crouching and looking at his bony hands. "On her bedside table. Under the base," he says, losing focus, "made of what?"

"*What?* I don't know *what*. What are you asking me?"

"A soft material?" he says, trying to snap his fingers and failing. "For the base?"

"Felt?"

He nods.

"Jesus, João!" You're yanking the trap door awkwardly upward, and flinging it among the statuary. The light from the window drives shafts through the gathering smoke.

"The thing is, one more thing: the legend needs a legend."

"The what?" you ask, tucking the rosaries back into your shirt; they're hot now against your skin.

"The legend for the legend is—"

You're looking for something to carry the ledgers in. "For fuck's sake."

João holds up a finger. He never cared to hear you curse. "See the father."

"The priest?" you ask, but again you know who he's talking about. There's always only been one priest. For João and for your mother. (For your father, not so much. He hated priests.)

"Go to confession," he whispers.

You're stacking the ledgers in the crook of your arm. "Fat chance."

"Tell the father that João told you to go to confession."

"You sound like my mother."

"Say it just like that." João swallows hard, fades for a split second, then comes back even closer to your face. "He'll lead you to the confessional. He'll know which one. Under the kneeling cushion: the legend for the legend for the ledger." He suppresses a bubble of mirth, a doomed giggle, then, his eyes brightening and wet, looks around one final time at this place, his home of 50 years. *It's history*, you want to say, but he already knows. *Kiss it goodbye*. It's already drifting darkly across the city. You look where he's pointing: but all around you, smoke is rising in gray tendrils from the seams in the attic floorboards.

Now you're kicking and shooing the volumes toward the trap door as they spill from your arms. You're dropping the books ahead of you, one by one, then to hell with it, just shoveling the pile into the hole. You're lowering yourself, hanging from the plywood, then falling to the linoleum of the top landing to see the flames gum and lap at the door frame. They spill outward and upward, blackening the ceiling plaster with staining liquid smoothness. Below you, on the stairs, the first-floor tenant: a young woman in a floral nightgown shields herself against the heat and dips her head to get a look into your face. Antonio's girlfriend. She's holding the nozzle of a garden hose stretched to its length. With every tug for more slack, the nozzle squirts into the wallpaper. And you see João standing in his living room now. He's surrounded by flames. Like a statue in a desecrated cathedral.

"Will I see you again?" you ask him, hesitating at the top of the stairs with your arms again full of his books. The question sounds childish and febrile, and you already know the answer. As you know the answer to any question you could ever ask him. There are no ghosts, and the only miracle is this: that there is something, anything, instead of nothing. You don't need ghosts, you need time. And luck. But you'll take the help anywhere you can get it.

Antonio's girlfriend is sobbing and yanking at the garden hose. She's like a ghost herself, a vivid spirit. And it shocks you to be able to see into the core of her being. That different kind of seeing you're prone to. Why now? Why anytime? Why ever? For a moment she's completely transparent. A timid soul pink-swaddled in a smothering corporeality. "Go," you say, your hand on her arm, which is shockingly solid and hot. She doesn't pull away; your touch seems to inject her with calm. What she says, you can't understand.

"No," you say. "Too late. Save yourself. Do it for Antonio."

At the name, she reacts in horror as you back away, down the stairs. Did she hear you right?

"For Antonio," you repeat.

The neighborhood dogs are massing along the street.

Following João's volumes, you go head first over the fence, rosaries madly dangling, a belly-scraping gymnasticism that brings the neighbors out screaming Portuguese. Dark old women pointing. So alive, you want to run to them, to shelter in their eyes. The wizened and the obese alike holding leaky buckets of water. Children dance around them like animals or insects. You stumble, roll in the grass, rise on your burning ankle to gather up the strewn volumes, and clutching them to your chest, you hobble along the driveway beneath the accumulating force of all those eyes. To the car. Touch-check the pistol in the front seat. Yes. It's all a dream. There is no other life but this.

3

YOUR WIFE. Your former wife. See her standing in the arched doorway of the two-bedroom cape where for ten years you lived with your two daughters. A long-term rental. You never owned it. A burning in your throat as you cross the little lawn, November dry. Even when it was green, you never mowed it. You hate lawns. You'd be damned if you'd mow what was never yours.

"I just got off the phone," she says, roughing you up with her eyes. Despite what you've come to think of as a recent thaw in your relations, you haven't seen her in weeks. Just this once, however late, you want to slip your arms around the woman, smooth her ass with your rough palms. But there's a strange next-level chastity between you now. Not a restraint—understandable given your history—a chastity. No other word for it. Last time you took your leave, you felt lucky, profoundly content, even blessed, in a manner consistent with your age, to part with a kiss. A kiss is no small thing. Now, you just want the animal smell of her neck. Her eyes won't have it. And—*wake the fuck up*—this isn't the time. "I just got off with Cindy." Cindy is Kelly's wife, your wife's cousin. A node in the inscrutable network.

You already know what that was about: the rumors of your death are making their way forth. The soon-to-be official news of your demise. They're probably on their way here right now. Berg and his Colombian associate. Forget your own apartment. There's nothing there for you of any value, never was. Talk a long look at this, you tell yourself, your home, or all the home you'll ever have.

Your wife pushes open the screen door. As you edge past her she snatches you by the elbow, her grip sliding to your wrist, halting you at the threshold. She's just looking at you with what you're tempted to call awe, but it's actually fear. Totally appropriate given the situation. It warms you.

You say, "Take the girls and drive south."

"You're on something." But she tightens her grip. "What's this got to do with me and the girls?"

There's no time for the usual pantomime. The stale performances. And you know she knows you mean business. You hold her gaze for as long as you can. Not so easy.

"You stink of smoke," she says, "and—"

"It's a cluster fuck." On the drive over, you were hacking

up gray phlegm, which you can still taste. You're not sure why you're whispering: "João's dead."

"That's what Cindy told me. Kelly's a mess."

"Yeah. He's got such a big heart."

"She said you and João went over the side two nights ago."

"And she was just getting around to letting you know."

She just looks at you.

"How's it feel to be a widow," you ask. "You don't seem too broken up about it."

"I just got off the goddamn phone. But I didn't believe it. She said you went over, with João."

"Not exactly. Though I did jump ship before they could do me."

"Do you?" A subtle turning and shift, and you can suddenly see into her varying depths—here just beneath the dermis to the grays and deep reds, there all the way through to the slick places that never see light. You might as well get used to it: it's back with a vengeance.

"They think you're dead."

"They know I'm *not* dead." You don't have to elaborate about who you really mean. It's all the same. The final five years of your marriage, she never pressed you on the extracurricular activities. The night work, whenever it was needed. Not often, but often enough. She went with the flow. Something you might have appreciated more at the time. You had it good, and the extra money, when it came, was always like a long deep breath of pure oxygen.

She hasn't let go of your wrist. There's a closed circuit between you, an errant electrical arc enkindled by the whiff and promise of violent death—yours—which is what you've been waiting for, after all, but which now only stirs a nausea in your bowels. They go hand in hand, death and its opposite. You've known one; you're curious as hell about the other.

You slip the vial of speed from your jeans, tap out four white pills. "Here," you say, rolling them into her palm. "You'll need these."

"Oh, really." She's been clean for a long time. She quit on her own, just stopped drinking the Chablis, which was her favorite. Cold.

"Take the girls. Drive south. Get on I-195 and go. Don't tell anyone. Don't call your mother. Just drive. Go now." You peel her grip finally from your wrist. "I'm not leaving until I see you on your way."

She scoffs, looks away, annoyed, but in the gesture you already detect a loosening. Her eyes have lost their power. "I've got work. I work, you know."

"Screw it."

"Right. Screw it. Easy for you. The girls just left for school."

You haven't seen them in a month.

"Well," you say, "pick them up. Go. Just do it."

She starts to ask you why, but she knows. It's simple math. She's the savviest woman you've ever known. The chickens are home to roost.

"Don't make me spell it out. Kelly's suppliers are rip-shit, they're in town and looking to clean things up. It's a problem."

"Where do we go?"

"What does it matter? South or west. Just keep driving until you can't drive anymore." You point at the speed in her hand. "Take as needed."

In the bedroom, where you don't even want to think about what's happened since it was your bedroom, you pull down her suitcase from the closet shelf and begin scooping the contents of her dresser drawers into it.

She's crouching to gather up what falls to the floor. She seems to be coming to her senses. "This is bullshit, you know."

"I'm not going to argue with you. It is what it is."

When the telephone rings, she stands up straight.

"Leave it," you say. "You need to be dead to the world for now."

"Like you?"

Your bitter grin. "I've never been more alive in my life." And you mean it.

"Cute."

From your jeans, you pull a fold of soggy hundred-dollar bills, the ones you found tucked into the back pages of João's final ledger. You count out five on the bed spread. "Take these. Drive south."

"Yeah, I get it."

"Check in somewhere."

"Then what?"

"Use your maiden name."

"No question about that," she says, leveling a frosty glare.

"Call me in a week."

"What if—?"

"Look, that's my plan. I'm freelancing here."

She's taken over the last of the packing now. Tucking, zipping. You're surprised at how easy this is proving to be, but you won't let up. Because it feels good to be taken seriously by this woman again. When she turns away, you glimpse once more the varying levels of her depths, as, passing in front of the glow of the desk lamp, her heart is illuminated, briefly, like the stylized Sacred Heart, a representation of which hangs on the wall opposite. You wonder why you've never told her about this—gift? No, you don't really wonder why.

"Don't call what's his name," you say.

"You know his name."

Actually, you've worked hard not to. "Whatever," you say. "Don't call him."

"Until?"

"No, better yet," you say, "call him first. Give it a week. Have fun with the girls. No one needs to know. Take them to Hershey, Pennsylvania. Go watch the Amish make chocolate. Normal tourist shit miles from here. Use your imagination. The fucking Liberty Bell. The beach."

"You're coming in loud and clear."

"Have him call me with the information. Where you are. If the son of a bitch can stomach it. I'll do my best."

Her head down: "So this is you taking care of us?" You meet her eyes with a chill. That tone she always used to shiv you good, with water-tight deniability. Such a skillful woman for so clueless a man.

"I wouldn't be here if I didn't care." You mean it. It's

obvious. "I want to see you go. I don't want to worry about you. One less thing."

"Can I take a shit first?"

"No," you say, trying not to smile. "Pick up the girls and haul ass. South. Now."

You want to whistle and shake your head in disbelief, because she's actually going. At the door, she pauses, points to the Jaguar across the street. "That yours?"

"Not bad, huh?" Then you give her a shove, the warmth of her shoulder blades briefly against your palms.

"Nice," she says. "Where'd you steal it?"

You stay behind, inside, with the door cracked, watch her manage the concrete stairs to the driveway in her threadbare jeans and jean jacket, lugging two suitcases. Now she's in the Civic and adjusting her seatback, now she's starting it, checking the rear view, backing squirrelly out onto the street. Now she is gone. Easy. You're aware of a howling behind your sternum.

In the bathroom, the hamper running over with towels, you snap on the overhead—it doesn't work—and look into the mirror. Your face streaked with smut. The nausea coursing through you seems only half physical. A deeper sickness. You gag, hack, spit. You twist on the faucet to rinse the wad of blackish phlegm away. You swab the sooty interior of your nostril with a finger of toilet paper. Flush. Swallow a mouth of water from the tap. Wait for the panic to begin to subside—it's the speed, it has your mind racing out to touch everything around you at least once—and rise to your reflection once more, your slack and stubbled jaw on a death head. A mug shot in an album of corpses.

Better flush that kind of thinking from your brain pain right now, asshole, that defeatist shit you're so good at.

With the ledger, you'll be trading for more than your own life. It hits you for the first time and you realize: it was always the case. Every step of the way.

4

YOU'VE NEVER BEEN INSIDE, which itself is a miracle. The Ash Street Jail. You parallel park the Jag on a nearby street with broken curbs, emerge with your eyes everywhere and João's last ledger tucked under your belt—you're not going to leave it. The pistol—that's another issue. In the streets there's a menace in everything you see. It radiates from the most mundane objects, from fuming cars with missing bumpers, from a length of black electrical wire blowing loose from a tenement's rooftop TV antenna, from unreadable bills stapled to telephone poles. The sun up now, weak through a layer of tissue clouds.

The jail is a redbrick affair from the previous century, a

lot like your grammar school, with dark acid-rain streaks like rusted iron arrows that narrow toward the foundation. With its grand entrance that anyone can walk right up to and knock on. Which you do. You knock and wait. A social call at the local jail. A little surprise visit. You knock again before noticing a small beige button like a door bell, which you ring. Nothing. You ring again, holding it a little longer. You try to settle your breathing. An alarm sounds, brief and dull, and the door begins to swing open on its own. You enter.

Along the hall, there's a key-scored Plexiglass window, behind which sits a woman at an electric typewriter, upright but fully asleep. She's in her early 30's, dark-haired and Portuguese, mustachioed, obese, pendulously breasted—and inexplicably you imagine her as your sleeping self, yourself as a passing figure in *her* dream, pale and doomed. You knock on the window, softly, and watch her surface into consciousness. See her eyes roll forward. She's looking directly at you, having remained completely motionless, her hands poised the whole time over the typewriter keys.

You tell her why you're here, to see Antonio, João's grandson, whom João and his wife raised as their own, and who is being held here largely for, as you understand it, his own protection, though nominally as a material witness in the DA's crackdown on drug trafficking in the city. As you understand it, Antonio began dealing for a supplier from outside the network Kelly hooked João into—a rogue sub-network broken loose to freelance. He was picked up, started narrating a story in the omniscient voice not only about his own supplier but the entire con-trolled substance distribution cohort as only someone in his position might know it. A great deal of the story was fiction, but he did provide—courtesy, many would assume, of his access to João's illustrated multiple-genre memoir—some useful information, and this is what set off the chain of events, communications, intimations, steely hints that resulted in João's being bound and thrown into the North Atlantic. The purpose of your visit? Good question. You're there on a promise to a fucking ghost.

You lie to the woman that Antonio is your nephew. When she hears the name again, her eyes widen for a moment. She half-whispers something unintelligible into a small microphone at the end of a flexible chrome stem, and immediately an alarm of deeper tone sounds and the sally port's gun-metal steel door, dense as a vault entrance and limned in chipped orange, swings slowly open.

The woman nods toward it. You thank her, but her eyes are already closing.

Inside the sally port, as the door edges shut, stands a small balding man in a dark green correctional uniform, about your age, whom, at the last minute, you realize that you know. You can't remember his name, but you can see through him, into the quick of him. When he recog-nizes you, his eyebrows flash, and a small glow at his core seems to whiten like an ember in a breeze. You knew him in high school. It's like a fucking class reunion.

"I'm not surprised," he says, patting you down.

"What, that I'm finally inside?"

"You're not in cuffs. That's a surprise."

Randall, that's the man's name, though you don't remember if it's his first or last. You were on the winter track team with him. He threw the shot put. He had a filthy mouth back then. It was ever *pussy* this and *snatch* that. A lot of talk about *nads* whenever he held the shot put.

"Antonio—"

Randall opens the inner door and you fall in to walk behind him.

"João's kid?"

You nod. You're tentative.

"You're not a priest, are you?"

"What the fuck does that mean?"

"I thought you might be here to give him Last Rights." The keys on his belt jangle as he walks. "Because he's as radioactive as you can get. The kid's all aglow."

He doesn't know the half of it—the glowing. It occurs to you that you never liked this guy.

He says, "He won't last a day on the outside."

"Yeah, well, we'll see."

Randall pulls up suddenly short, a bitterness around his mouth. "He won't last a day on the outside," he says again, slowly this time. "There's been a change of strategy. You think I don't hear things?"

"I have no idea what you hear."

"He'll be out soon."

"Got it." You want to reach in to his inner ember and yank it free. "You going to take me to his cell or not?"

He leads. You follow. The layered cells and mesh catwalks rise to a skylight three stories up, dingy light filtering in. It's like an elaborate verdigris bird cage. Folded hands, wrists resting on the cross irons between bars. The only faces you see are when someone angles a mirror in your direction, and even then, after a flash, all you get are tight-framed eyes. As you pass, the chatter quiets. Like respect for the dead. It picks up again only when you're further along.

In a room barely large enough to accommodate a plastic table-and-chairs unit like something from a school cafeteria, Randall invites you to sit. You remain standing. Randall shrugs, takes his time, steps into a small bright office, comes back out with a sheet of paper, throws a pen on top of it. "Sign that."

You sign it. "That was easy."

"Follow me."

You do, out another door and along a dimmed corridor past a bank of cells with two or three dark men each, whose eyes follow silently. "You're not his first visitor today," Randall says. One of the men colorfully curses Randall, who makes a raspberry sound with his lips and laughs without lessening his pace.

"No?"

"Mendoza."

"Mendoza? What was that about?"

"The fuck would I know?"

At the end of the corridor, he turns to fumble a key into the door, and when you catch up with him you see Antonio lying on a small bed with his back against a paint-flaked wall. He's older now, but vividly recognizable as the kid who would sit for hours watching João and you play chess. Flickers of João—that kindness, that softness—in his face and hands. The sight of him there, alone, abandoned, the cell the size of a bathroom, catches you by surprise—the cruelty and blind inevitability of it. Not until you've stepped into the cell and Randall has locked the door behind you, do you feel the confidence to speak in an even voice.

"Back in ten minutes," says Randall walking away. "Have a nice chat."

There's no place to sit. Just the bed, a stainless steel toilet without seat or cover, and a few scraps of paper and illustrations and photographs cut from magazines taped to the high walls. The walls are so high, the room so narrow, it occurs to you there might be more living space if it were tipped on its side. There's no mirror, just the polished surface of blunt aluminum screwed to the wall over a sink.

"I'm here to tell you something."

Antonio snorts, swallows, but says nothing. His face is blank. Like João's minus the wisdom now.

"I'm a friend of your father's."

His brow bunched: "My what?"

"João."

"He's not my father."

"You don't remember me?" you ask.

"I didn't say that."

"Good," you say. "Look, there's no other way to go about this. I'm just going to say it." When you do, Antonio's expression doesn't change. He just keeps staring at you with his lingering sneer, though the cost of maintaining it may have changed. "He asked me to visit you. To let you know."

"Got it," says Antonio. "He asked you to let me know he's dead."

You can't answer that without revealing your own tenuous grip on reality. "Look, I know what it's like—"

"What what's like?"

"Losing a father." It's a lie. You don't know what it's like. Not like this. Maybe you know how losing a father thrusts you into another realm, strange enough. But you want to assure him that it's not so simple, that he's not actually responsible for his father's death. Not technically.

"I just told you, he's not my father." Suddenly, he seems about to lose it, which terrifies you, and you take a step back, literally—as far as space allows—and begin examining what's taped to the walls. "So you can get the shit out of your ears."

"Why was Mendoza here?" you ask, nonchalantly as you can.

"You got nerve."

"I won't argue with you on that score. What did Mendoza want?"

"What the fuck do you think?" he says. "You're late with the news. Congratu-fucking-lations."

"João loved you."

Antonio blows air through his lips, shakes his head, his eyes squinting at you from the side. He seems about to rise. "And so I ask you again: what the fuck is that to you?"

You almost tell him about his apartment. How it's not there anymore. He couldn't have heard that news. But something has your attention—something taped to the wall near a dog-eared centerfold of an impossibly large-breasted woman: a birthday card. It's homemade, more of a birthday painting. Aware of Antonio's eyes on you, you move closer. It's one of João's, a small watercolor on salvaged butcher paper—one of his favorite media—folded over for delivery but subsequently spread flat again, its crease smoothed over with a greasy palm. The face of Jesus looks off to the left, as though contemplating the reclining nude on the wall nearby. He's done up like an old icon, blocks of Byzantine color behind him. The eyes wide with shock or rage. Not an illustration you yourself would choose to accompany cheerful birthday saluta-tions, but—

"My birthday's in August," says Antonio. "A father would know that. I got that yesterday."

"Yesterday?" You're right up on it now, no way to hide your fascination. "Do you mind?" You run a finger behind one of the edges, lifting to reveal a hem of letters. "I'm going to take this down," you say, and begin peeling it from the wall.

"Sure," he says, "help yourself."

You turn the painting over, strip away the loops of tape, refold it, then push against the crease to bow it out and match up the obverse edges of the short sides of the rectangle. There. The figures align in perfect correspon-dence. One line of letters, one of João-like signs and sym-bols. You smooth the fold firmly and pull the ledger from your belt with your other hand.

"Have you seen this before," you ask Antonio, holding it up.

"Are you done? Because this Q-and-A? It's bullshit."

You compare the writing. No doubt about it: the legend for the ledger. Or one of them—for the legend? You feel a surge of annoyance at João, tuck the folded painting into the ledger, ask, "Can I take this?"

"Anything to move your nosey ass on out of here," he says. He never liked you. "Is there anything else I can help you with?"

"When are they letting you out?"

"How is that any of your business? Not to repeat myself."

You say something you've never said before, not sincerely at least. "Look, Antonio, it's going to be OK."

"Oh, is it?"

You smile. It's like you're on something. You are on something, which is making you lightheaded even now, and the room seems to jump-cut back a millimeter or two without anyone's notice but yours. "Guaranteed."

"Man, that's a relief."

It's true. They're not going to touch him. You know this. You can't see into the kid—your inner vision, as ever, unpredictable—but you can imagine his, João's, descendants populating some fucked-over, otherwise unimaginable future world. A world you may never see. They don't look happy, but they've survived. The meek shall inherit, etc. A nation unto João. You call for Randall, immediately hear his keys jangling against his meaty thigh as he approaches.

"Question," he says a moment later, out in the hall: "Who the fuck is Randall?"

"That's not your name?"

"Fuck you," he says, locking the door. "Once an asshole always an asshole."

You glance back into the world of Antonio's tiny cell, meet João's eyes in the body of a terrified child. The slender fingers and wrists and delicate elbows. Something beyond knowing there. Beyond your knowing, anyway. "It's going to be OK," you tell him again, a blossoming in your lungs as though it's João's voice, not yours. "Trust me." But there's no response.

"That's funny," Randall says further down the hall. He's not smiling. "How you can joke at such a moment about such a thing."

"They're not going to touch the kid," you say. At one time, you thought you were related to this man, whatever his name is. Distant cousins from the illiterate, inbred crossroads of French Canada. Quebecois. Different branches of the same family come south to work in the textile mills. But he's so wizened and sour, you find it hard to believe now. Then again—

You step out of the sally port, then turn to watch it slowly close on the man, who will come no farther. His white core is dimming, filling over with sinews, with adipose, with capillaries like unknowable networks and maps. With dermis. "The kid's days are numbered."

"No more than yours and mine."

"No more than mine, maybe," he says, crossing his

beefy arms. "Yours?" He's grinning beneath a sly brow. "You don't have much time."

"I don't need much time," you say. "Whichever way it eventually works out, I'm good."

Randall just stands there with a look on his face that suggests you're an idiot, or at least someone who walks around posing idiotic questions, which, for his money, is the same thing. The door is almost shut. "I want to wish you luck."

"What's stopping you?"

He just goes on staring at you, but all the life has gone out of his face.

Sitting in the Jag, you're absorbed with lining up the symbols on the back of the water color again and double-checking them against those in the ledger. That's when you notice there aren't any numbers. There are numbers in the ledger—all those sums and figures—but not in the legend. That's not the only thing you notice. You're just a noticing machine today. There's a slip of white paper under the Jag's windshield wiper. You get out to lift the wiper and you read what's printed there: HAVE YOU VOTED YET? It's a flier from the League of Women Voters. That's right: it's election day in America. Then you notice something else: *Call Mndza*, written in shaky pencil, and there's a number. Standing in the street, your eyes everywhere, the speed having steeped your nerve cells, you're picking up that radiant menace again, much more vivid now. It's coming off all manner of things.

5

DEFUNCT SERVICE STATION on Kempton Street. A gouged pay phone. You back in beside it and crank down the window, lift the receiver to listen for a dial tone. You slip a quarter into the chrome slot—it's all sprayed over with flat black paint, streaked with flame-shaped burn marks—and dial the number and wait for the connection to be established, the faint scent of shit or piss or vodka issuing from the mouth piece. You're patient for the telephone at the other end to begin to ring. It erupts like some snoring beast as someone picks up, but then there's silence. Fifteen feet away the wind pastes a Burger Chef sandwich wrapper to a chain-link fence. Beyond, a trash lot with spectral, knee-high Queen Ann's

Lace, and cloud shadows that sweep and crawl at angles over melted vinyl siding and clots of colorful car parts. You close your eyes and the silence opens up, visual and real. You replace the receiver, sit there watching an elderly couple leave what you take to be a polling station in the basement of the Orthodox church across the street. Voters. People having voted. Having cast votes for one or another candidate. Freshly smug with a sense that their choice ever mattered. Their choice. The telephone rings, and you raise yourself to lift the receiver again, then settle back into the bucket seat of your stolen Jaguar.

"Wish I had better news," says Mendoza. He sounds sad. You know he and his wife recently moved to the north end, but you don't know where, though you assume it's somewhere in same world as the one you currently occupy.

"We'll look back on this someday and smile."

"They just want the ledger."

"I'm aware of this," you say, checking your teeth in the mirror. You need to brush. You're suddenly aware of your exhaustion. You could close your eyes and leave the conscious world behind. "And they're going to get it."

"That's good to hear." Mendoza's voice brightens artificially: "Might be wise to make that sooner than later."

"I'm not their fucking errand boy. There's a price attached."

"Shit," says Mendoza through a surge of static. "Let's not complicate this."

"I hear you. It's complicated enough. Still—"

Mendoza clears his throat, shifts the phone to the opposite ear.

"On top of everything else, it's unreadable," you tell him. "You can't read it."

"Maybe *you* can't," says Mendoza. "Is it in Portuguese?"

"Not the parts they'd be interested in." You notice one of the voters staring your way. He's standing among a gaggle of proud Americans. He taps his wife on the shoulder, says something, points, and begins his approach. An oldster in a vest.

"So you're picking and choosing?" Mendoza asks. "Here's an idea: just hand over the whole thing and let them sort it out."

Something about the way he says this registers darkly with you, even above the nascent anxiety you've begun to associate with the approaching voter. What the fuck does he want? You feel for the pistol under your seat.

"Who's there with you?" you ask.

"What the fuck does that mean?"

"It's not in Portuguese, Mendoza. It's in João's secret code."

Mendoza cups the phone and says something over his shoulder. You can't hear what it is. You're holding the gun just beneath the window. The man has stopped next to one of the abandoned gas pumps. He's wearing a vest from a three-piece suit. He looks like a tailor. Twenty feet away now, he's padding his pockets like he's lost or forgotten something.

"You know nothing about this?" you ask.

"João's code?" says Mendoza. "No. Not officially."

"I'm not sure what that means, but maybe that's why I'm not there right now. I intend to deliver it with the legend."

"Unwise complications."

"Could be, but that's where it is."

"Understood," he says. Then, nonchalantly: "And where are you right now? Physically, I mean."

"Like you have no idea," you say. "You left me that note."

"What note?"

Now the man in the vest is bent over at the passenger's-side window, waiting, patiently, to speak with you. When you look over, he knocks, unnecessarily. You make no effort to hide the pistol as you lean to roll down the window. "What can I do for you?" You're annoyed.

"Nice car," he says, sliding his hand over the curve in the driver's-side door. A cliché performance meant to communicate nothing more than how little he appreciates small talk. He's got more important things to communicate. On his vest, a sticker reads I VOTED TODAY.

"Thanks." The receiver cupped against your thigh, the gun in your other hand on the wheel, you just look at this guy. "It's hot," you say. "Stolen."

The man's jowly face drops. He shrugs. "It's still nice." Up close, he's a rougher-looking customer that you imagined. A retired alcoholic bank teller with a strong sense of civic responsibility.

"Anything else I can help you with?" You point at the phone.

He nods, but with a hurt expression.

"Tell them if they're willing to pay," you say to

Mendoza, "I'll give them the works. Ledger, legend, the whole goddamn works."

"How much are you asking?" Mendoza says, a little too quickly. "Not that I've got some kind of hotline to these assholes."

"Mendoza, cut the shit." When the man at the window finally notices the pistol, he straightens, pushes back from the car, shoves his hands in his pockets, and beelines across the cracked parking lot.

"What does that mean? I'm just asking."

"I'm interested in living," you say. "Same goes for my wife and kids." You almost add *and Antonio*, but you don't want to push it.

In the long pause, you listen for what might emerge from the silence behind Mendoza. Finally, he says, "Are you sure you know what you're doing?"

"No," you say, your eyes closed. "Are you?"

"I ask because, on the level, there's a man with a semi-automatic weapon sitting on my couch right now. He hasn't stopped talking about you."

"Does it have one of those banana clips?"

"Is that what they call it? He's just talking away. He took off his flip flops when he came in, and I got him a beer. He won't put the gun down. Otherwise, he's a friendly enough guy. He can't say enough about you."

"Thanks for finally getting around to that important bit of information." The alcoholic bank teller is back among his cohort. He's pointing your way, and the gaggle is watching now, like a crowd of geese all pointed in the same direction. "Want to put him on?"

Mendoza covers the phone for a moment; then you hear Berg's falsetto. "Well, hello, friend."

You don't say a word.

"We need to catch up on things," he says. "Think you might have some time to swing by?"

"Love to, Berg, but I have a few concerns to take care of."

"Industrious you," he says. The archness in his voice needles your anxiety.

"How does it feel to be back in town?"

"In beautiful New Bedford? I have to be honest with you, friend, I haven't missed it even a little, even with all its—I'm looking for a charitable descriptor here—*texture*?" Berg is pleased with himself. "I've thought about you often, though. Our lengthy discourses."

"That's ancient history."

"I wish we could have one of our sessions right now, talk it over as in the days of old. I feel I have a lot to share with you."

"What about?"

"The nature of things," he says, swallowing, "the many epiphanies I've had. It's been an interesting ride, I can assure you." Berg yawns, loudly. "But, I don't know, there's always been something missing."

You hold off as long as you can: "Such as your soul?"

Berg bursts out laughing. "Oh, that's rich," he says, "coming from you."

"Is it?"

"And a little disappointing. You were never one of those holier-than-thou types. It was one of your few saving graces. You were always so sympathetic. What happened?"

"What happened? Your boys murdered someone—"

"My boys? Murdered?"

"Yeah," you say, staring in the rearview mirror at your hollow eyes, "someone I loved."

"My boys murdered someone you loved."

"Is there a better word for it?"

"How about occupational hazard?" he says, his voice leveling out. "Speaking of which: Do you have the ledger?"

"I do indeed."

"Is it as—comprehensive as it's rumored to be?"

"Yes," you say, "but it's useless as is."

"Oh? Pray tell."

You give him the barest explanation: the need for legends, alphanumeric and otherwise. He's attentively verbal. "I see," he says, finally. "Here's a thought: let's pool our efforts, make use of the myriad resources at our disposal. Let's work together."

"I want to deliver it complete. I have a feeling it's the only card I have left."

"Wow. The only card," says Berg, dreamily. "That sounds like it means something, but—"

"You tell me. You're in the business."

Berg covers the phone with his hand, says something unintelligible to someone in the room. He comes back all business: "Where are you right now?"

"Physically?"

"Did your final visit with Antonio go well?"

Before you can answer his question, the receiver issues

a resonant synthetic tone, followed by a mechanical voice, unnerving and vaguely female; it asks for you to please deposit 35 cents. Before it can repeat the request, you hang up and swing the Jaguar out of the parking lot and onto Kempton Street.

The gaggle of self-satisfied voters is on the move, walking in pairs along the wide sidewalk and engaging in animated post-poll discussion of the kind imagined by denture cream advertisers and the otherwise brain-dead. One of them, a thin woman in a vintage dress, is wearing Uncle Sam's top hat. You slow to their pace, roll down your window, wave the man in the vest over to the curb. But he's not coming. He's a nervous wreck. "What?" you say. "Come here." The small crowd veers away onto the lawn of a ruined mansion. "Just for a second." You want to ask them all not just who they voted for, but who's on the ballot. Of this you have no clue. At first you're nonplused, annoyed—even offended—at their reluctance to share such neighborly information. Then you realize you've been waving them over with the loaded pistol.

6

 THE ATTENDANT is a flaccid man in flimsy, loose-fitting synthetic materials. His name tag reads WALTER. He's sitting behind a huge oaken desk with a green-shaded brass lamp and eating a salad comprised of numerous cold bean varieties from a lidless Tupperware bowl. When he notices you standing there, he seems annoyed at the interruption, a white plastic fork in his fist.

"Busy day for Agostinha," he says, though you've only identified her as "João's wife." He looks you up and down. "Let's go," he says, his jaw working.

The hospice is dark—and Catholic. Death is everywhere. In the cracked discoloration of the mint green wainscoting. In the dull hallway floors reflecting window light, the light itself laying it down like a thick lacquer. You drift past doors thrown open onto doomed villages of motionless men and sightless women, not all of them old, though all at various stations of departure. A sense of cold pride moves through you: who else but the Catholics could understand such nuances. Their strong suit and their trump card—death.

João's wife seems dead already. She lies with her hands folded over her stomach, an intravenous tube looping from a chrome tree on wheels to the place where it enters her bloodstream, held tight with a beige strip of surgical tape. The crucifix João referenced back in his attic sits on the table beside her, but you keep your cool. You tell Walter you have some news for her. "It's not good news." Then kick yourself for being so dramatic. You took another of João's white pills on the drive over, and its magic is being born again, radiating out into your system. You're trying to pace your words, to keep them from running into one another like boxcars, to sound like a normal human being. It's not easy.

"Oh?" he asks. "I'm so sorry to hear that."

"Think I can be alone with her for a minute?"

"Of course," he says, a little offended. "What relation are you to Agostinha?"

"None," you say. "I work with her husband."

"Another coworker." Walter smoothes the bed spread over Agostinha's knees. "It's like Grand Central in here today. How is João?"

You search his face for a sign, for nuance, see none, then imagine the old man's shade standing in the center of his fiery living room. "Same as ever," you tell him. "You know João."

Walter's tone takes on an edge of vacant reproach: "He hasn't been in for a couple of weeks."

"But it's been busy?" you ask. "Today?"

"Relatively speaking."

"Who's been in, if I might ask?"

"Never seen them before. I don't know them. Cousins, they said. They didn't stay long."

"Oh? How many of them were there?" you ask, trying to keep it together, let the words emerge at their own pace. "Was one for them a scrawny little asshole with stringy blond hair?"

Walter looks up at you with alarm, his posture stiffening. For a moment you think he's going to open up, reveal himself, inner light and vitals and blue sinews. But no. "I'm not sure if that's any of your business," he says frostily. "Even if it were, I'm not at liberty to give out that information."

You want to slap the officiousness out of him. You imagine doing it, the tussle that would follow, right here among the dead and dying. Instead you motion to Agostinha. "How's she doing?"

Walter just continues to stare at you until the question registers with him finally, like sound catching up with light. "She's comfortable."

"How can you tell?"

"In the drawer—" he slides the top one open, then shut—"you'll find some of Agostinha's books. João reads to her. When he's in. Stay as long as you like."

"Thank you, Walter."

He looks directly at you for a moment. "They're in Portuguese." He leaves.

There's a heavy wooden chair facing Agostinha's equally unresponsive neighbor, who doesn't seem to need it, so you turn the chair around and sit. João's wife doesn't stir or even flutter her eyes. She doesn't appear to be breathing. You resist going for the crucifix, survey the large room, an act of nonchalance for no one in particular's benefit. Everyone there is either asleep or unconscious or dead. Hoping to see something deeper but knowing you won't, you train your gaze into the core of this woman, João's wife of decades. She's never been one to open up to you in that way. There's only darkness. It doesn't work like that, anyway, doesn't arise on demand. An utterly useless skill.

A voice breaks in over an intercom affixed to the middle tile of the dingy drop ceiling. It's an elderly voice, with a restrained eagerness and excessive purity of tone that strikes you as either the epitome of sincerity or a soul-crushing performance. Can you tell the difference anymore? The Lord's Prayer commences. You remember you're wearing João's rosaries, and you stand to slip them over your head, then coil the beads on the side table, and, in the same beat, lift the crucifix, and sit back down. You turn the little metal sculpture over; the felt padding isn't there; it's still on the table. In the metallic recess of the base, there's nothing, just rough metallic plating in concentric tarnished circles. You reach for the felt padding; written there in pen, barely readable: *And whosoever was not found written in the book of life was cast into the lake of fire. Revelation 21:10.*

Blankly you sit there. What does it mean? You scan the room. Nobody. Just the rows of beds, most of them empty, and a half dozen black-and-white TVs with monitor-burn mounted big above the room. A morning broadcast news show. The familiar footage of the student raid that began the Iranian "hostage crisis" one year ago today. Smoke drifting into the streets outside the embassy. The blind-folded American diplomats and embassy workers in their wide belts and bell bottoms, the radical students in too-large military field jackets and too-small v-neck sweaters. You can't hear the audio, but each TV is tuned to the same station, giving the impression that the image, reproduced six or seven times over, is stationary and the room itself jittery and shifting. It's like that at sea sometimes.

You tuck the felt padding into your jeans and rise to approach one of the sets, craning your neck as you do. The national news anchors—those genetically engineered morning show people—are talking up the elections; the polls are open. You can read their lips. They're about to "throw it over" to the local affiliates. You can feel it coming. You know what you're about to see. The image on this particular set begins to roll, rapidly. When it stops, just as suddenly, you see an image of yourself; set next to a tightly cropped, washed-out Polaroid of João, it's an overexposed black-and-white shot from when you were in the service. Why that photo? Of some stranger, someone so completely not-you as to make you smile.

It's just so—ridiculous. The words MARITIME MISHAP underneath the two photos.

It's official. You're dead.

A woman in a bed across the room wakes in a vicious coughing fit. She lifts herself abruptly on her emaciated elbow, her fist to her mouth. With each hack, she grows more desperate, until she's gasping. When she spots you, she raises an index finger, as though calling for a check. You want to help her. You hesitate. There's no staff, no one else vertical but you. The intercom prayers have moved on to the Hail Mary. The woman sounds horrible. What can you do? It's the agonizing struggle of the drowning. You find yourself moving across the room and leaning over the bed, one hand in hers, squeezing, the other hand smoothing her sharp shoulder blades. You're lip-syncing the words of the ancient prayer, as though you were its delivery system, your eyes stinging. She's not as old as she initially appeared, maybe mid sixties, but pallid, skeletal, her eye sockets bloated with edema. Anyone could see she's in the final days, maybe the final hours. Finally, exhausted, her breath still cluttered with phlegm, she collapses into the pillow and squeezes the moisture from her eyes, then opens them to lie staring up at you, blank, unsmiling, her chest working, her hand still in yours. You're ashamed because you don't know what to say. As if there were words. Your own face is burning. As the prayer comes to its conclusion—"now and at the hour of our death"—you look away. On the TV a commercial for Dr. Pepper is playing out like a musical number without music.

When you start back toward João's wife, someone is sitting in the chair beside her. You stop short, stunned: it's the father. A black bag at his feet. His palm on the back of Agostinha's hand, a small viaticum kit arranged efficiently on the bedspread, gold pyx and oil stock and carefully folded purple stole. You drift closer, thinking you could slip past the man, but you just watch him as he lifts the crucifix on the bed stand, upends it to check the bottom. When he sees the felt pad is missing, he looks around. When he sees you, he doesn't seem surprised.

"I have it," you say.

"You have what?"

You approach. You pull the felt padding from your filthy jeans pocket, unfold it, and hand it to the man. Reluctantly he takes it. He reads what's there, his face unresponsive.

"And who are you?" he asks. You're stung that he doesn't know your face. It can't be.

"João's friend."

"João's friend," he repeats, flatly. You haven't see the father in years. When he first moved to the parish, you still lived at home, with your parents. He visited your mother often: he was young, smart, even charming in that way priests can be. Witty, knowing. Something off limits about him. His eyes always sizing you up, taking your measure—and your mother's side. Later, in the months after your father's death, he was back. This made perfect sense to you: he and your mother shared the same broken knowledge of things. A kind of language. Years earlier, you'd walked in to see them sitting silently in the dark together. On opposite sides of the room, the light low, the darkness of a density commensurate with their silence. They weren't praying. Whatever had happened between them—if it even had—that was over, history. Even so, the priest's attitude toward you changed after that night. That you didn't seem to mind at all, whatever the case had been, whatever it looked like—that's what really seemed to change him. What kind of a son? Etc. When she died, your connection to the man narrowed to João's occasional references, "the father" no closer to your immediate experience than João's lost old country. Seeing him now, you're confronted with time's ravages. How little choice we have. He's in his mid seventies, with the wide florid face of a professional Irish drinker, lumpy and red-mottled with rosacea. But he's thin as a refugee, not an ounce of fat on him, his hands an assortment of largely obedient bones. But they shake, the impression one of ravenous hunger. He sits there searching your face, as in the days of old, waiting for some sign of what you know, what you're worth. A familiar searching. A sounding out. You're an expert yourself, given a mirror and an empty evening. He has his secrets on you as well, though you've never had reason otherwise to question his commitment to the vocation. It's dark enough for him.

He looks at the felt padding again. "Did you write this?"

You shake your head no.

"Does João's friend have a name?"

"He does," you say, "but he's a shy man."

The father folds in two, then hands you, the felt

padding, and you slip it back in your filthy jeans. "That's not Revelation 21:10," he says. "It's 20:15."

"João's dead."

"Yes." He looks away.

"Word travels fast."

"Trite but true."

You're trying to see through it, whether it's an act or not. All of it. Any of it. You motion toward João's wife. "I came to tell her."

"Is that all?"

"No, it isn't all."

"Do you want to talk about it?"

"That depends," you say. "When I think about what happened to João—"

"What happened to him?"

"He's dead."

The father nods. "A good man."

"You think so?"

He rises to his feet, attends to his viaticum kit. You step back, beyond an ancient imaginary circle, watch him slip the stole around his neck.

"Don't let me interrupt," you half-whisper. "I'm on my way out." He lifts a finger without turning. Wait. He unscrews the lid to the oil stock and prepares to perform the ritual of extreme unction—if that's still what they call it—upon Agostinha. It doesn't take as long as you remember.

When he's finished he stoops to lay Agostinha's left hand where it was, on her right. Like some funereal statue from the Dark Ages.

"João recommended you to me for the sacrament of penance," you say. It sounds rehearsed, insincere.

He's folding the stole now. "Did he?"

"He said to ask you to hear my confession."

"Yes, the terms are synonymous."

"I'm following his instructions."

"You were his friend," he says, "after all."

"Father," you say, reaching out to the man, your trembling hand like something apart from you. Animated by something other. "I'm scared."

He glances at you with a look of annoyance, and you let him take you by the elbow, steer you out into the hall, past the legions of the doomed, past Walter, who's finally finished his bean salad. Walter nods. "Fellas," he says, without affect, "you have a wonderful day."

In a corner of the parking lot, after the dim interior, the mid-morning sunlight pains the roots of your eyeballs. "They burned down João's place," you tell him.

No response from the father. His own eyes seem to search the gravel at your feet. He's a tight package of reticence and mystery.

Finally he clears his throat. "You haven't changed, have you?"

You remember looking into the man, or trying to. He would have been someone to confide in, back then, but he was dark himself. He's still dark. "You certainly have."

"More than you know."

João had hinted at certain dark developments in his recent relationship with this man, and with the history of the church João attended for 35 years. At the time, you hadn't paid these hints much mind. You didn't care.

"I have the ledger," you say, then lift your jacket to slip the notebook from your waist band. "I saved it from the flames."

The father avoids looking at it, carefully raises his eyes to yours, as though to comment on such a portentous phrase. "Let's take a ride," he says, gesturing toward a blue Buick Skylark at the edge of the lot.

"You haven't seen my new set of wheels," you say, pointing at the Jaguar. Then you waggle the ledger. "You don't recognize this?"

"What do you want me to say?"

"Whether you have any idea what's in it, father. For starts."

"I know João had a talent for illustration. For detail and description."

"It's written in a secret code."

"Neat."

"Father, I'm lucky to be alive."

"If only more people felt that way."

The smug son of a bitch. But you keep it together. "João suggested you might be able to provide me with the legend—or at least one of them." You gesture for him to take the book. "That you might lead me to it."

He finally does, take it, reluctantly. *"Lead you to it."* He begins to leaf through its pages, comes immediately to the legend and the remaining hundred-dollar bills. "What do we have here?"

"One of the legends," you say. "That's what he called it."

As the father fingers the bills, the morning sunlight reveals, over his nose and cheeks, a vast web of capillaries. "Why do you need any of this? What's the plan?"

"The plan, father?" you reach to take back the ledger, but he won't let go. "To sell it."

Frowning, he asks, "What's the asking price for something like this?"

"The lives of my wife and kids," you say. "My life. Antonio's life." You start to tell him about Kelly and night work and the last trip and the taped-up packets of weed and waking to find João gone overboard and your miraculous cold-water swim to shore. But the father doesn't seem to be listening. Finally, as though giving in to some voice within your voice, he stops you.

"You're not telling me anything I don't know," he says, almost brutally. "So let's cut to it. What's your timetable? Is it tight?"

"Pretty fucking tight, yes."

"You're supposed to be dead."

"They're looking to make it true." Your peripheral vision narrows and there's a simultaneous humming from far away that takes up residence briefly in your skull, like a compact swarm of killer bees, and you feel as though you'll pass out, there in the gravel, face first. "I need the legend for the legend—yeah, can you believe this?—so these assholes know what I've got is legit. Does that make sense? Otherwise, it's just a bunch of squiggly lines."

"I understand, " he says. "Are you armed?" He's so matter-of-fact about it.

"What the fuck kind of question is that?"

"The practical kind. These are rough characters you're dealing with."

"I have João's pistol. He seemed to know what was coming."

"That fancy thing? Novo Estado? That antique?"

"You're familiar with it?"

"Of course," he says, starting for the Jaguar. You follow. "So you're carrying?"

"Do I have it on my person, right now? No. I didn't think it in good taste to visit a cancer hospice armed."

Calmly, the father sets the black valise on the hood of the Jag. He opens it, fishes elbow-deep among its depths, produces a silver revolver, shiny in the sun. "I lost any such scruples a long time ago." It's a nickel-plated thing.

You don't know what to say, speechless at the image of your mother's favorite priest standing there with a .38 caliber handgun. It's not exactly pointed at you, just trained low and in your general direction. You raise your hands.

"For God's sake, put your arms down." You do. He tells you to get into the driver's side. You do that too. He gets in. You start the car. There's a nurse smoking a cigarette and eating a bagel as she leans against the redbrick. She doesn't seem to notice or care that you're being kidnapped. You pull away.

"Where to?" you ask, pausing at the entrance to the lot.

"Holy Family Church," he says. "Of course."

"Are you insisting, father?"

Suddenly shy, he sneaks a glance at the revolver in his hand, still held low. If it went off, you'd be minus a knee. "I am."

7

YOU THREAD THE JAGUAR through the dissolving
neighborhoods, in their midst the great granite
churches like desiccated shells. As you pass, it all glimmers and fades. Visible from many blocks away, the
father's church, your mother's church, your church, seems
to be the exception. The way it went from the French
Canadians and the Portuguese, to newer immigrants, the
Vietnamese and Guatemalans. He did it all, the father,
kept it going, counseling, providing drug services, bap-
tisms, RCIA, learning the languages as needed. How? It's
obvious, at least in part: Because of people like João.

Now he thumbs through the ledger's gray pages,
his revolver forgotten between his legs. Not exactly a

dangerous man—or dangerous for reasons not so obvious. He's got João's watercolor, the first legend, spread out as well, and he's absorbed with working through João's private code.

"They're related but they don't exactly match up," you say.

"I can see that."

"The one legend deciphers the code; the other, I'm guessing, the names. I'm guessing it's all numbers."

"Let me ask you a question," he says, finally.

You're dizzy with fatigue and hunger, navigating a wilderness of stop signs. "Shoot."

"How do you know João's dead?"

You're just looking at the man.

"How do you—" he starts again.

"I heard you." For a moment, the man seems to open up. You think you catch glimpses of the scenery passing behind him, like a lake or ocean caught sight of through dense forests. "Are you asking if I saw it happen?"

"Did you?"

"I told you, I was sleeping." You're suddenly exhausted. "He was gone when I woke up. On deck, nobody could look me in the eye. Kelly, Mendoza were all tight-lipped and noncommittal. They couldn't answer a straight question."

"That's it? That's all?"

"This was night work, father," you say. "You're familiar with the term?"

A ripple of annoyance. "Who do you think you're talking to?"

"We were in the middle of the North Atlantic. When someone's suddenly not on board and there's two guys not from your crew in fatigues carrying rifles with banana-clips—"

He's staring past you. And you realize for sure: he knows all about this kind of thing. As João's confessor. He knows more than you ever will.

You ask, "What are you suggesting?"

"Nothing," he says. "I'm trying to connect the dots."

"The dots." You pull into the parking lot of Holy Family Church, ignore the parallel lines, and kill the ignition. Four or five cars scattered about. "What do you know? Tell me about those dots."

The father gets out of the car, then you get out, and you follow him across the parking lot. "It's election day," he says, nodding toward an elderly Cape Verdean woman in finery coming out of the church basement at the far end of the parking lot.

"Isn't that exciting."

"Did he ever talk about the old country?" he asks.

"Yeah. All the time. The apparitions. The agents from the Vatican."

"Of course," he says, without turning back. "That's it?"

"No, that's not it, but—"

"Nothing about Tarrafal?"

You shake your head, but he doesn't see it. It's a lie anyway. You've heard the word before—another door opening up, but only for a moment, into something too dark for words. You never pressed it.

"Nothing about the Campo da Morta Lenta?" he asks,

then seems to regret it, quickening his step. The Camp of Slow Death. You have just enough Portuguese to remember the phrase.

The narthex of the church is dark, as cold inside as out, colder. There was a time when you imagined what they said was true: that God himself dwelled in the little gold house beyond the altar rail. But no one seemed to make a big deal of it—other than to kneel now and then. In your dreams you stood barefoot before the tabernacle as it opened slowly, liquid light pouring forth, the face of God just about to be revealed, always on the verge, whereupon you, your smoke-stained soul, when it happened, would disintegrate before its blast of cleansing energy. There'd be nothing left.

The father motions for you to follow him through the sanctuary, to a small office off the sacristy. You do. On the wall, a portrait of the baby Jesus titled "The Light of the World." The same print hung in your home as a child, but you never liked this Jesus. He seemed a competitor for the precious little oxygen of your youth.

The room smells of mold.

The father flips on the fluorescent overhead, sets the valise on his desk, motions you to sit in the one of the mustard-yellow fabric chairs.

"I appreciate the hospitality, but—"

"Sit down," he says, laying the revolver on the desk. He pats his pockets, finds a crumpled packet of Marlboros, a neon-green plastic lighter. He doesn't speak again until he's taken a drag of his cigarette. "Did João tell you why he emigrated?"

You feel yourself growing arch and impatient. "I assume for the same reasons anyone does."

The father's expression has changed. He's smiling, if only to himself.

"He spoke of you often."

"Of me."

He nods.

"Can you hear my confession now?" you ask.

He leans forward, his hands on the desk top. He seems about to say something of catastrophic importance, but it's only: "Follow me."

Out in the main cathedral again, your footsteps echoing on the marble. All this space, so empty. You wonder how many parishioners still come to Mass. You follow the father's smoke trail along the peripheral aisles to one of the large confessionals: a heavy wooden box between heavy red curtains that wrap around a small dark place to kneel. The father turns, raises a finger.

"Let's make this count," he says, "given the circumstances."

Your last time at confession was an unpleasant experience. You'd been attending other churches, up in Taunton or Braintree, anywhere but here. But when it came time for the sacrament of penance, when it became unavoidable, you didn't want to run from him; you knew he'd recognize your voice. It seems so pointless now. The rites and forms. This was back, years before your daughters were born. The need for absolution concerned, among other things, your wife's abortion. You'd been visited by night terrors, your sheets damp by four every morning, a blue-black world scraped clean of any comfort, her breathing form inert. If that wasn't hell, you don't know what hell could be. The darkness writhed around you. It hadn't been just her decision. You'd decided together. And you'd driven her the three hours to Albany, New York. You wanted the father to have something on you now, something your mother could never know. A simple exchange. A gift and a symmetry. This was back when people spent a lot time thinking about such things.

You don't even have to speak.

"No," he says, softening, "let's make this count."

"Where's your .38 when you need it, father?"

He smiles and shakes his head slowly. "Please," he says. "Don't make me appeal to you mother's memory."

"I won't. I appreciate it."

"It's important," he says; then you think you hear your first name, but the acoustics in this cavernous place have always been questionable. "To me it is."

"Sort of a before-battle kind of thing?"

"I need to ask something of you, too."

You feel carried along, a weakness.

"Forgiveness for what I'm going to do," he says. "Which is let you to walk out of here."

"That's not your choice, father."

"I led you to the legend," he whispers. "This is madness. I didn't have to."

You can see it now: a minor glowing as of light behind a frosted glass, wavering but persistent as an electric bulb in one of the burn-safe votive candles behind him. The idea more than the thing itself. But you're so exhausted, so burnt crisp by it all, you're not sure of anything. You've been talking to the dead, for Christ's sake, taking instructions from the other side. *What we come to.* But then maybe this is how we disappear from the world: gradually, hour by hour, person by person. *Don't push it away, don't shit on every last thing of value.*

"Let it be on me, father." You surprise yourself by taking his hand, which is warm and damp. You know it all now. How lucky this man is to have had principles to compromise, to have loved something beyond this world by loving something *in* it. By loving *through* it. A way of being you might have even aspired to yourself. "I know it's not a pure thing."

His grip tightens in yours. "Is anything, ever?"

"Thank you for not asking me to go to the police, just for the charade of asking me."

He takes a sharp breath; it lifts his shoulder. "There's another thing I need forgiveness for."

"From whom, father?"

"From your mother."

"Just her?"

His eyes dart to the altar, then back to you. "Let's make it count."

You remove João's whale tooth rosaries and hold them out for the father. When he sees them, when he realizes what they are, he flares back for a moment, fades, but then seems to rally enough to move forward again, vaguely. He takes the beads and, head bent, disappears into the middle door of the confessional, the one between the hanging curtains. A gaudy red light—like a glowing ruby ring—goes on above. You obey the signal, part the curtains, kneel. The little lattice door between you slides open.

"Run your hand under the kneeler cushion," he says in a whisper. "Then we'll begin."

You do what he says, your fingers breaching the napped seam left and right, then up against a slim bound notebook, which you pull free. It's small enough to fit in your jacket pocket. There's another of João's pills in there. You take the opportunity to dry swallow it, feel it scrape along the length of you.

"Got it," you whisper, feeling yourself about to rise to leave, but you don't. You stay, as though having reached the limit of a tether. "Bless me father for I have sinned—"

"Wait," he whispers. "Please." For a long time, you kneel quietly, listening to your own breath, and the sound of the father weeping just inches away.

"It's OK," you whisper, barely audible to yourself. "Father, please." When he stops, you begin again: "Bless me father for I have sinned—"

In the darkness, the smell of his cigarette breath. Candle wax. The residue left behind after holy water evaporates. The silence that makes your words possible. At first, you give him a list of fodder, what you think he's expecting. The litany too dull to report, a series of painful clichés. But soon you're lost in that darkness, speaking into a void as lonely and profound as the one within which you fought for breath, struggling for the surface. Not a body. A voice.

You finish. The father whispers your penance. You walk

to the front of the nave to kneel before the altar rail. The sense of space is overwhelming, as is the feeling you're on the verge of evaporation. It's absence and presence both—as though the distinction means nothing. Into that silence, you pray your penance as fervently as you ever have, half-listening for the father's footsteps passing.

You half-raise your head to see him donning his vestments, watch him retrieve a host, readying it at the altar. You're looking into another world. He works quietly, efficiently, then rounds the altar to approach with the ciborium, a segment of the Eucharist already lifted. But before he can say the ancient words, he pauses. He's looking past you to the rear of the church. You want to turn, to see what he sees, but you can't. "The body of Christ," he whispers hastily and places the host on your tongue. That taste of foamy nothingness. He takes the rest of the Eucharist himself, chews it on the way back to the tabernacle. Then, his face overcome with confusion and fear, he waves you on—"Quickly!" You rise to follow him, trying to make as little noise as you can.

He waits for you to enter the sacristy with him, the gold-thread in his vestments trailing light, then closes the door behind you. He holds up a finger again, his head cocked, his eyes widening. He's afraid but, closer now in the light, you see that he's also excited, his chest rising and falling. A hollow sound above the marble spaces of the nave. Clear and distinct. Quickly, in exaggerated pantomime, he's into his valise. Now he's holding the revolver low against the side of his leg. It's surreal. "Where's your weapon?" he whispers. You realize it's still in the glove compartment. Another echo, voices. You're chanting *pray, pray*, in your mind. *Let's see what you can bring, father.* He shrugs a question at you: *All set? Got what you came for?* You tap the notebook in your pocket, nod. You hear cursing in the church. The father turns off the overhead light. He's focused now, sweat glistening like the gold-thread as the voices grow louder, rough voices calling out, delighted at the echo they're making.

"Go," he whispers.

You shake your head. *Fuck no.*

"Go!" He waves the .38 toward the tiny bathroom. "The window."

It's almost funny.

There comes a heavy crash from the church, a series of concussions, a mighty issue from a baseball bat striking wooden pews. Stomping. Swearing. Whistles. Hoots. The father doesn't have to ask again. You're in the bathroom, the flimsy door shut behind you, the ancient eddies of holy water and melted paraffin on the air as you crank the window lever; it opens with a sucking sound like a tomb—wider, wider. Not wide enough. You're up on the tank of the toilet now, the porcelain slippery and unstable beneath your boots. The voices louder. You imagine the father wasting one them. Would he shoot low? Or pop the motherfucker in the face? Now, finally, there's a pounding on the door to the father's office. You hear his voice call, "Yes?"

All unassuming.

More pounding. "Fucking open it!" It's Berg, his laughter resonating.

You punch through the screen, rip it free, and force the window off its extender. It swings open to smash against the brick exterior but won't come free of its hinge, so that as you struggle through the opening, you're half in, half free, writhing like a maggot, when the office door explodes just beyond the bathroom door and you can hear the father yelling, his voice as guttural now as the others. As male. With the sound of the first shot, you're tumbling forward onto the concrete of the walkway, your pant leg having caught for a moment on the extender before tearing free, a gash opening up in the white flesh of your calf. Sweet pain, clear and sweet. You hear yourself curse. The ledger in hand, the rosaries free from your shirt and slapping your chest. *Kill me now and I'm good to go. Straight to heaven. Bring it on. I welcome it.*

The Jag is pinned into its space by an idling U-Haul van. You haven't even pulled the door shut before you're wrenching the gearshift into reverse, stomping the pedal, bringing all twelve cylinders to bear on the rear quarter of the big U-Haul, a crunching squeal as sickening as it is satisfying—forward again to the concrete curb segment, then back, T-boning the motherfucker, again—twice, three times, you've stopped looking. Bam, bam.

Through gritted teeth, you're babbling: "You picked the wrong asshole to fuck with!"

The pistol in the glove compartment, now it's in your free hand, you've got it out the window, you're angling impossibly backward, you're pulling the trigger, the recoil about to break your wrist. What are you firing at? You glimpse your own eyes in the rearview—wide, wet, alive. You wheel into a reverse arc back into the lot just as two men burst from the side doors of the church, their flip flops slapping, and of them is Berg, and his feet slip out from under him, a shotgun in one hand, the AK-47 in the other, and he goes down hard, you see it through the windshield now, his head bouncing once in the grass. And you're so cranked on speed and your own adrenaline, you're steering for them both. *Fuck with me?* But then there's the father right behind them. See the man down on one knee in the door frame, both hands on the shiny .38, its muzzle flashing as he squeezes off shot after shot, rounds going everywhere, grazing the U-Haul, one of them skipping across the cracked surface of the lot and taking out your rear window. You laugh at the chaos, at the thought of one of the father's errant rounds passing through your skull—then where would you be? And all this gunfire is enough to send the other motherfucker scrambling into a row of hedges—along with half a dozen old guys just now emerging from the polls beneath the church. Clear of the U-Haul, you've half a mind to swing back and run them down—Berg and the Columbian, not the elderly voters, you'd spare them—and you go so far as to jump one wheel up on the curb, but then you straighten out to watch in the rearview as Berg rises to his knees with the AK, and you motor off into the neighborhoods.

8

K ELLY DOESN'T KEEP his doors locked. He lives in a subdivision where this isn't necessary, with long artificially winding streets without curbs that end here and there in neatly tarred turn-arounds. His house is of recent construction, with a pretentious palladium window and a long driveway. It's set on an angle back on its own acre and half of rich dense lawn, still green even with winter approaching. You leave the Jag on the frontage road, make your move. But for the faint rush of the highway, everything is quiet here. It's easy to cross a stretch of field, Johnson grass switching your knees, then cross at a lope into Kelly's backyard with its bright plastic jungle gym, swings, a tree house halfway up the only tree.

Fucking thing even has electricity, an orange extension cord running from it to the cellar bulkhead.

It's just as easy to walk into the kitchen. You're not noisy about it, but you're not particularly quiet either. You close the screen door behind you, you don't slam it, then turn to see Cindy standing with a gallon of milk in one hand, the brushed-chrome refrigerator half open. She's a small woman with the greyhound physique and the well-considered hair of the leisure class, someone comfortable with the envy of others. She's your wife's cousin. You know her from brief encounters at family reunions and, of course, as Kelly's wife. Sometimes she'll pick him up at the docks in one of their cash-bought cars, drive away without a word between them.

"Hey," you say, trying to slip the pistol into your jeans at the small of your back. She's seen the gun, so there's no reason to do so.

"Hey," she says.

"Kelly in?"

"He's still sleeping."

"I'm going to wake him."

She hasn't moved. "OK."

You take in the kitchen, the high ceilings, everything new and clean. "Nice place." The kitchen in your apartment isn't large enough for two people, which you've convinced yourself isn't a problem because no one has ever visited.

"I know," she says. You're feeling a little dizzy. Oddly, despite its size, you seem too large for the space, as though you've lost track of where you end and where the world begins. There's a drop of your blood on the tile floor. As Cindy closes the refrigerator door, you catch a glimpse of the countertops behind her, just a glimpse—straight through. They're granite and lit by a lamp tucked up underneath the oak cabinets. You watch her lungs fill and empty, fill and empty. They're bright and look like flaming wings, and their flaring seems to register your shame. "Don't worry," you say.

She shrugs, stretches a grin. "How are you?"

"It's just—"

"You don't look well."

"I appreciate your honesty."

"Sorry about your mother," she says. You haven't seen Cindy in a while.

"Thanks."

"Kelly's down the hall," she says, motions. "He's sleeping."

"How are the kids?" you ask.

"Good. They're at a friend's house."

You feel a wash of relief at that news, liquid weight streaming from your body. Their kids—you forget their names, would forget them immediately if reminded—attend private school, which Kelly has always had a problem with, afraid they'll grow up soft. But really he's pleased because, like the Lincoln Continental with the opera window and the new air-conditioned pick-up in the driveway, this all speaks to the kind of social status that owning several fishing vessels affords. But Kelly doesn't own several fishing vessels. He doesn't need to.

He's locked into other revenue streams. The fruits of his skill set.

You nod, take a breath as quietly as you can. There's blood in your boots. It's your blood.

"How are the girls?" she asks.

"Fine, Cindy." You motion down the hall, as though you'd like permission. "Thanks for asking."

"Kelly will be glad to see you."

"No, he won't." You're standing about 15 feet from her. She's wearing a set of red sweats, tennis shoes, and a white head band. "But don't worry."

"I'm *not* worried," she says, surprise coloring her voice. You almost believe her.

Beneath a mirror sits a beige telephone on a small table-and-chair unit in the hallway halfway to the bedroom. You avoid your reflection. "Is this the only telephone in the house?"

"No. There's one upstairs."

"Is anyone else upstairs?"

"No."

"No kids?"

"I told you where they were," she says, almost annoyed.

"No Spanish-speaking men in fatigues and flip-flops and dirty white socks?"

Cindy laughs. "What?"

You adjust the gun in your front waist band and pick up the telephone, receiver and all. "I appreciate your honesty, Cindy," you say. "I always liked you." Chilled by your choice of verb tense, you test the length of the cord, fight the urge to rip it from the wall.

At the end of the hallway, you nudge open the door with your foot to find Kelly lying on his side, his eyes just opening. They take a moment to focus, on you. He doesn't sit up right away. He just watches you. "Fuck me," he whispers.

"*Que pasa?*"

He swings his legs over the edge of the bed and sits up. "And what can I do for you?" He's a large man, Scotts-Irish, with a huge head and close-cropped hair and a perpetual 10-day beard you're surprised someone like Cindy allows. He's barrel-chested. A body for making abrupt contact, as befitting an enthusiast of the sport of Danish kings. He played hockey in high school. He's always been among the toughest, if not the toughest in the room. But he never had much luck with the women. Not until Cindy. She was, according to your wife, the first woman to pay him any attention. And they've been married for a long time. Both graduates of the public school system. Kelly's done all right for himself.

Trembling, you set the telephone down beside him. You don't know how this will go, if you'll be able to speak straight. You part your jacket to show the handle of your pistol above the waist band.

"Oh," Kelly says, "it's like that." He looks past you at Cindy, but you're not concerned about her. She's still standing next to the refrigerator. You don't have to turn around to know this.

"Don't worry about your wife." You motion at the beige telephone with the pistol, which you're suddenly holding. "I need you to make a call."

"I think I can do that," he says, looking at the weapon again. "To who?"

"To whom," you say. "We're going back to sea."

Kelly scratches the underside of his beefy arm. "Are we?"

"I've got something for your boss."

"My what?" He begins to open up before your eyes. And you're thinking, *shit, not now.* "I work for myself, asshole." Ribs, sternum, his aorta shuddering. You've known him for years; this is a first. You want it to stop. There's a good chance you're going to kill him. You'd hate to watch him die from the inside out.

"I've got something for your boss."

"I have no idea who you're talking about. And you have no idea what you're doing."

"Shut the fuck up and call." You can feel the weight of the gun in your hand now. Your every joint is aching. You want to pop another pill, but you can't remember where they are.

"And say what?"

"I'll leave that to you. This ends today. I'm willing to barter."

"With what?"

You lift your shirt and pull free the ledger. Hold it up.

"Nice," he says. "João's fucking ledger."

"Call them. Use the magic word. This is what they're after, right? What they've been tearing the shit out of everything for. What they burned João's house down for."

He shakes his head. "You watch too many movies." When he stands, and you raise the gun to belt level, he puts his hands out. "Take it easy, asshole."

You point to the phone again.

"You think I can just dial them up? It's not like that. They're not sitting around a fucking telephone waiting to hear from the likes of me. I need a radio. We'll have to go down to the *Pio*."

"What about these assholes running ragged all over town?"

He shrugs. "It's a free country."

"Fine," you say. "Get dressed."

You watch him slip on his jeans, pull on a sweater, step into a pair of well-worn loafers. "This is going to end bad," he says, "the way you're working it."

"Wait," you say, pointing at the telephone again. "Call Mendoza."

"Why?"

"Because he's coming with us."

"Why get him involved?"

"He's already involved. Call him."

Kelly sits on the bed, lifts the receiver, hesitates, then dials. The sound of the rotary spring uncoiling in the dim room.

"Mendoza," says Kelly into the receiver. "Your buddy's here."

You turn to see Cindy standing at the other end of the hall. She's occupying herself with the thermostat.

"He wants you to come along," says Kelly into the phone. "Tell me about it. The man's on a mission. He's one doomed motherfucker, but what can you tell a guy like that?"

You signal for the receiver. "Hello, Mendoza?"

"Yeah?" His voice is strained and frightened.

"Meet us at the *Padre Pio*," you say. "I need a second hand."

There's a silence on the other end.

"Come on, Mendoza," you say, looking at Kelly, who's smiling now. "Think of João."

"Don't say that."

"Mendoza—"

"What are you asking me to do?"

You hang up. "He's coming," you tell Kelly. "We're on."

You wait for him to edge past, then follow along out into the kitchen. Slowly, he puts on his grimy Mackinaw jacket, his eyes on Cindy. "Leave this to me," he says to her. "Me and him are going to work this out."

"I'm sure you will."

"Don't call anyone. Sit tight. Lock the door after me. Call the Larsons, tell them—or *ask* them—if the kids can stay there tonight."

Cindy is taking it in, nodding. She's a cool customer.

"This isn't something to get excited about," says Kelly.

"I'm not excited," she says.

"He's just upset about João." Then, with a trace of mockery: "The man was like a father to him."

Outside, the pistol held low, you shadow him along the driveway to his pick-up truck. It's a bright day. Election day. A Tuesday. The world drenched with the mundane.

"Did you vote yet?" you ask him.

"You're really going to keep this up? It'd be a shame if that gun went off accidentally."

"It would be fitting. It's João's piece."

You and he get into the cab at the same time.

"Put it away," he tries again, "seriously. You're not exactly a comforting presence, with your crazed eyes and a gun you don't know how to use. Really. It's not necessary. We'll work it out." He's about to turn the ignition.

"Like you worked it out with João?"

He shakes his head. He turns the engine over, then pulls forward across the sidewalk to roll through the neighborhood's winding streets.

"You have no idea what you're into here," he says, finally.

"Yes, I do."

"These people are out of control," he says. "It's not just Berg, either. I'm not sure how they found out, but they're obsessed with this fucking ledger."

"Bullshit. *How they found out?* How else would they find out?"

"I tried to tell them it's a whole lot of nothing. That Antonio's just a punk. That he's not worth the fucking trouble."

"Is that what you think?"

"I don't care."

"I do."

"Look at the man's heart bleed."

"Shut the fuck up."

For a moment, he seems to be calming down, but then something sets him off, and he's getting more agitated again with each stop sign. "What's the plan? You just hand over the ledger and then what? You're not thinking. What then?"

"I walk," you say. "They get what they want. Everything

goes back to normal." But he's right; it makes no sense. You're talking out of your head. You put your hand on the ledger in your lap. "This buys me some insurance."

Kelly slams the wheel. "You stupid shit."

"Maybe."

"No, not *maybe*. These people, they're a fucking force of nature. They're not going to differentiate between you and me and—. This fucks us *all* over. Me, Mendoza."

"Antonio."

"Are you kidding me? In this town? That kid's already as a good as dead. There's local concern. These guys don't even have to lift a finger on his account."

"What about me?"

"Ha! Are you serious?" He looks over smiling, almost warmly. "Kiss your ass good-bye."

"I'm not worried. I'm already dead."

"You stupid shit. Just give it to Berg, for Christ's sake. He'll give it to whoever."

"*Whomever*," you say. "That would be stupid."

"Any stupider than this?"

"Lose the attitude. I'm all cranked up on João's speed, I'm unfamiliar with firearms, I've just been to confession. The body of Christ is making its way into my system."

"Fuck you."

Dockside, the *Padre Pio*'s bilge drains noisily from its bright blue hull, oil spangling the surface of the harbor.

"Anyone on board?" you ask as you follow him over the gunnel.

"Fucked if I know. It's not my boat."

"You got that right."

"Look, I'll try to hail them," he says. "I can't guarantee they'll be available."

"Just tell them we're coming, with the ledger. They were heading north when we met them last time, they've got to head south sometime soon. Mention the ledger and they'll free up their schedule."

"Who's this 'we'?"

"You and me and Mendoza."

He throws his hands up. "Bull*shit*."

"How much fuel do you have?"

"Not enough," he says. "Just give the fucking thing to Berg."

"I'm not trusting it to the errand boys."

"Call Berg that to his face and see how long you continue to breathe." Suddenly, his concern strikes you as genuine. "I think that might be the best offer you'll get."

"Where are they, Berg and his friend, anyway?"

"I'm not their fucking supervisor."

"Use your contacts, Kelly. Call the mother ship. Set up the rendezvous. This is nothing new for you."

Kelly looks around as though for help. You follow his eyes, count it as another miracle that there's no one in sight. "João made the choice himself," he says, checking his watch. "He knew what he was getting into."

You're in no mood to discuss João's moral choices with a man at least partially responsible for his death. You stick close behind Kelly as he crosses the deck and climbs the bridge ladder to the pilot house.

"Mendoza's on his way," you tell him. You have no idea if this is true.

"Not if he's got a brain in his head, he isn't."

Up in the wheel house, you point the gun at the radio set, and Kelly says, "All right! I got you," then starts in with the tuning and the frequencies, technical skills you've never bothered to learn. Again and again, he issues mic clicks into the ether.

"Is that all there is to it?" you ask. "How's it going so far?"

"Did I not tell you it would be hit or miss?" He finds a loose cigarette on the dash above the dials and gauges. "May I?" he asks you. And when you nod, he lights it up and takes a draw. "Stale as shit," he says.

Behind him, what looks like Mendoza's Gremlin is turning from Route 18 through the gates to the docks. The car slows to a stop, then just sits there.

"It's him," you say, but you're not sure.

Kelly turns. "Madness."

The door swings open and, like an angel, Mendoza steps from the car. "See there?" you say. Sheepishly, he comes forward with an AK-47 slung over his shoulder. He's alone.

9

NO ONE SPEAKS for the first 30 minutes, the 24th hour of your ordeal having come and gone. You sit behind Kelly as he mans the wheel, trying every few minutes to raise the supplier on the radio. The moon has risen in the day-lit sky, its pale cream reflection on the console through the eastward windows. Kelly looks at you for a moment, then back, before saying, "OK. I'm going to need one of João's pills."

You hand him the vial and he pops two of them, lifts and shakes a number of soda cans on the dash, seeking one with something left in it. Finds one. He washes the pills down.

"They don't have their ears on," he says, grimacing with distaste.

"I hate that bullshit lingo," you say, raising the pistol. "Keep trying."

"Yes, sir," he says. "You're pretty fucking brave with that piece."

"Brave enough."

Mendoza stands in the bow, leaning into the breeze with the Kalashnikov still over his shoulder. Like a down-in-the-mouth Nicaraguan contra. He hasn't said much. He seems caught between opposing forces. You think of a term João might use: *spiritual warfare.*

Kelly hawks and spits on the floor of the pilot house. "I can't believe I'm participating in this ridiculous excursion."

"Let's hear what happened to João."

"So now you want the truth," he says. "Well, it's inexplicable. The truth often is."

"Unreal."

The radio crackles twice—the sound of a distant microphone being keyed in rapid succession.

"Answer it," you say.

Kelly picks up the mic, but that's all he does.

"Answer it."

He clicks the mic twice. Then a voice comes over the radio. "What's the word, Kelly?" It's Berg.

"He's sitting right here."

"What the fuck?"

"Yeah, he came to *me*," he says, looking at you over his shoulder. "With the goods. We're headed out for a meet.

He's got this master plan. He's all convinced of several things that bear no relation to the world you and I live in."

"Why doesn't that surprise me? He's an idea man. Always was."

"He thinks they're going to sit down and bargain with them," says Kelly. "You know them better than me. Are they people to bargain with?"

"Doesn't that beat all?"

"You with Blue?"

"He's sitting outside in his damaged U-Haul. It's totaled. Your man's got no respect for private property."

"OK, Berg? Let the word go forth. He's not *my man.*"

"Oh?" Berg's tone is one of barely restrained glee. "I wouldn't have had the pleasure but for your intervention."

"I just work with him." Kelly looks at you again. "*Worked* with him."

Berg cackles. "He's losing friends left and right."

"Can you set something up?"

"Who with?"

"See, that's what I've been saying. But he's got his heart set on it. He wants a meet. And here's the thing: we're low on fuel."

"The silly fuck."

"He insists," says Kelly, turning to look at you. "And he's armed."

"Tell me about it. He's a fucking army of one. Him and that gun-wielding priest."

"What does Blue have to say?" Kelly asks.

"Not hard to guess, but I'll seek his advice."

"Let him know how it stands," says Kelly. "I'm under a little duress here."

"Blue's got a fairly precise idea of what we're dealing with."

The radio squelches into silence.

Kelly snorts and shakes his head, his anger flooding back with a kind of rancid laughter. "The shit storm you're calling down on yourself. Your wife, your kids. Me, Cindy. Mendoza and his family."

"You ever visit João's wife?"

He glances back at you. "Is she still alive?"

"You're a champ," you say. Berg's voice sounds again from the radio. You're on your feet and up against Kelly's side now, pressing the barrel of the weapon into his love handles.

"Surprise, surprise," Berg sings. "Blue says it's on." Then he reads off a set of coordinates that Kelly jots down on a pad of paper.

"That does surprise me," says Kelly. "This ledger has them seriously spooked."

The tone of Berg's voice suggests a wide smile. "Blue's enthusiasm for this is rather high."

Kelly turns to you, winks. "Really?"

"His only regret is he won't be there for the fireworks."

"They're not upset?"

"Did I say that?" Berg coughs, mics out, comes back on. "Now you're sure he's in possession of the McGuffin?"

"The what?"

"The ledger, friend. The reason anyone is even bothering to rouse."

"He's got it stuffed into the front of his pants."

"Eew. Not the most sanitary mode of transport."

You snatch the mic from Kelly, who steps back from the pistol. "Berg, hey, hello, asshole. Tell them what I'm in this for."

"Can you fill me in?" asks Berg. "Because I'm at a real loss. I have no idea what that might be."

"Total severance."

"Total what?" Berg is laughing in cartoonish falsetto. "What the fuck does that mean?"

"I'm out," you say. "For good."

There's a long pause, while static, the echo from the world's creation, sizzles just below the squelch. "Roger on that, my friend," Berg says, his tone liquid and mockingly official. "I would assume they're arranging for such an outcome as we speak."

10

BEFORE DAWN, Kelly throttles down the *Padre Pio*, and it settles forward into the ghost of its own momentum. As quickly as the engines die, a kingdom of silence reigns. Still dark. No sign of another craft. Venus in the east bright as a distant spotlight. The seas glassy.

"Take a look," Kelly says, nodding at the fuel indicator, the dial a hair's breadth below E.

"Noted."

"Happy now?"

"Elated."

"So how is this going to work?" he asks. He's trying to be sincere, but it's hard for such a sarcastic man. Even so, there's a sub-current of concern in his voice, as though he's already nostalgic for your lost companionship, for the man he'll still be when you're no longer the man you were. He's clearly exhausted, but no one's as exhausted as you. "What's your hustle?" he asks.

Mendoza appears at the bridge ladder but lingers in the threshold of the pilot house.

"I have no idea."

Kelly turns to Mendoza: "Care to inject some sanity into this? Tell him how insane it all is. Or have you got religion too?"

"It's all insane," says Mendoza, parroting Kelly's tone. His face alternates between scraped-out horror and unnerving blankness. "I have no idea why I'm here."

"Because," says Kelly, "you're not a complete asshole."

"Thank you." Mendoza's voice is faint and hollow. "My wife might take issue with that."

Kelly's expression changes. He steps forward to lift the rosaries you're wearing. You tense up, but there's nothing overtly hostile about the gesture as he rolls the beads between his fingers, frowning his cigarette downward. He seems about to sniff them, but instead lets them drop, scoffs from the back of his throat, shakes his head again. Pure Kelly. "You think these are going to save you? You think God's looking out for you?"

"It can't hurt."

"Oh, yes, it can," he says. "By making you stupid brave. What are you, six years old?"

You tell him they were a gift from João.

"What'd they do for him?"

You hear the North Atlantic, placid as lake water, lapping at the hull.

Kelly leans an elbow on the control console. "You think I don't know you?" he says. "I'm married to your wife's cousin." He slaps at Mendoza's shoulder. "I been hearing about this guy for years."

Wide-eyed, Mendoza continues to stare at a spot of discoloration on the floor—spilled coffee, a stain in the shape of Maryland or Rhode Island. From the first days of the *Padre Pio*. João tried to bleach it out, but the faint outlines remain.

"We *were* related by marriage," says Kelly. "But the man fucked that up too. He's skilled at fucking things up. It's like his life's mission."

"Anything left from the last trip, to eat?"

"I'd be more than happy to go look," Kelly says, bright again with malice. "Isn't that why I'm here? To cater to your every fucking need?"

"Aren't you hungry?" you ask.

"Yes, I am, because when I wake up after a long trip, I eat breakfast, unless of course there's a clown standing over me with a pistol. Unless I'm kidnapped."

"What else would you be doing today?"

Kelly stops, seems ready to hold his peace. "I should fuck you up for that alone."

"Just go check."

"You trust me?" he asks. "Out of your sight?"

"I shouldn't, but—"

Your fatigue has taken on new shadings and dimensions, expanding beyond who you are, opening out into space. It comes in swells that crest to leave you wallowing in numbed valleys. Try as you do to fix Kelly in the center of your field of vision, he seems to drift lazily one way or the other.

He says, moving closer, "Put the fucking piece away, will you." Then he squeezes past Mendoza, stops, slaps him on the shoulder. "You too, for Christ's sakes. It's bad enough. I mean, ain't we mates?"

Cursing softly, Kelly descends the bridge ladder. And you wait for the newborn silence to mature between you and Mendoza. You ask him, "Why *are* you here?"

"I thought you could use my help."

"I'm sorry for pulling you into this. Where'd you get the gun?"

"Berg and his friend left in a hurry."

"It looks good on you."

"Yeah, thanks," he says. Then: "I had nothing to do with João. I woke up half an hour before you. He was already gone."

"So you're really here for João? For some payback?"

Mendoza raises his eyes slowly.

"The man loved you, Mendoza."

"Not as much as he loved you," he says, quickening. "I mean it."

"Bullshit," you say. You know it's true, but you're ashamed at this pointless accounting. You're not brothers, you and Mendoza.

A minute into Kelly's absence, the radio registers five rapid dead-carrier mic clicks, like short sandpaper strokes on brittle plastic. You don't say anything, but when it happens again, Mendoza looks sheepishly at the radio. The sea air washes in through the open hatch.

You say, "What do I do?"

"You're asking me?"

You detach the mic from its clip and respond to the clicks with five of your own. If it's Morse Code you have no idea what you're saying. You flunked that course in basic training. If there ever was one.

Kelly is in the pilot house again, two sandwich-sized objects wrapped in aluminum foil in one hand and three bottles of beer warm in the other. "I don't know if this is still good," he says, peeling back the foil. "Turkey. Does that meet with your approval?"

You tell him about the dead-carriers.

"What'd you do?"

"I clicked back."

"Outstanding." He twists open one of the beer bottles. "Eat up. Because I believe it's your last fucking meal on Earth. Maybe ours, too, you crazy—" He finds the binoculars and stands with his legs apart scanning the horizon, or as much as the pilot house window will allow. While you've been occupied, something has materialized from the bluish black to glimmer weakly in the west, then goes dark. Kelly points at a small green smudge on the radar. "Shit, here they come."

A surge of stomach acid to make you swoon. Mendoza slides the rifle from his shoulder, holds it away from himself as though he's never seen it before. He detaches the clip, checks it for rounds, fumbles to reattach it.

"Answer me this," you say to Kelly. "Did you just stand there when they did João?"

Kelly tries to speak through a mouthful of turkey. He glances at Mendoza, who's retrieving the clip from the floor. "You're so woefully misinformed about the nature of things," he says to you, finally. "Pathetic."

"That's always been my Achilles heel."

"Yuck it up," he says.

There's just enough daylight to discern the approaching craft. Wide and shallow, its bow rides high and smooth in the calm seas, the rising light, the rhythm of its hull reaching you in abstract, disembodied percussion. Four figures hold fast to different points: one at the wheel in back, one standing at the bow, two more men seated in the middle of a wide bench. Out of the pilot house now, Kelly, Mendoza, and you watch in silence as the boat banks into a curve at 150 yards, circles twice, then suddenly falls from its orbit, throttling down its three powerful outboard engines. Inertia carries it forward to where it bobs and wallows alongside the *Padre Pio*, both craft facing north.

"I want to see your bullshit world view shaken to the core," Kelly whispers low and vicious. "Your confidence and your rosary beads and your self-righteous fucking indignation."

"No more little white pills," you say. "I'm cutting you off."

It's dark, but not dark enough to cloak the old man. All four men are standing now, João unsteady but surprisingly lithe for a man his age. He's staring at up you, frankly, as though from across a gulf. Wordless, apparitional, smiling sadly.

"So, asshole," Kelly says, smiling with glee, his hand on your shoulder, squeezing, "what do you have to say now?"

You shake him off.

"Look at me," he says. He's trembling.

Mendoza is coughing, hacking, as though ready to vomit. "What the fuck?" he manages to say.

You? You're not so sure. "That's not João."

"Isn't it?" Kelly slaps your back. "You clueless fuck. Look at him. Who else would it be? Wake the fuck up." He comes alive suddenly, waves down at the boat. "João, what's the word?"

You hold up a hand as though to silence Kelly. In it you're clutching the SIG Sauer P226.

"Is that wise?" Kelly hisses at you. "Flashing the piece? Use your head."

You're trying to hold it together, a rush of thoughts you need to stop up and reverse and send back through in some kind of order. "If I want advice from your sorry ass, I'll ask for it."

"You wound me," Kelly says, laughing.

You call over the rail and across the void, "Good to see you, friend." Your voice is high and unnatural. Unsteady. "I have something of yours."

One of the men leans to whisper something to João, who nods gravely, then whispers a reply. Over the gulp and suck at the *Padre Pio*'s water line, he calls to you: "Do you mind if I come up?"

"Just you?"

"Well," he says, shyly, "me and my friend, Mr. Salazar, here." Mr. Salazar nods a greeting your way, his eyes wide, and smiles into the *Padre Pio*'s deck lights. "He's anxious to make your acquaintance."

You turn to Kelly: "What should I do?"

"You are a piece of work," he says. "Unbelievable."

You turn to Mendoza: "Thoughts?"

Mendoza's no more helpful than Kelly. And you struggle with the urge to rush forward and slap the useless expression from his face.

The light is rising by the minute. Salazar and the two other men are armed. Salazar wears a pistol holster over his form-fitting knit sweater. He's a muscular man. The others, both heavier, darker, shorter, hold much more imposing weapons—one a rifle of some sort, the other a black sawed-off shotgun; they're being careful to point them nowhere in particular. You strain to see if João himself is armed—whether that's a holster on his belt.

"Come on up," you say to João. "It's your boat."

João grins faintly and reaches for the rope ladder. Up he comes. He's followed by Salazar, then one of the other men. You drift back, your mouth dry, as you watch them climb. It's amazing: the closer João gets, the more radiant he seems to grow. But it's the simple radiance of being. Nothing more. At the top of the ladder, he winks. With this and the obvious stiffness of his bearing, it occurs to you that *It's all an act. They're holding him.* You're thinking, *when you move, move quickly, move decisively, without warning—if you move at all.* You know enough to take advantage of the one thing on your side: being absolutely fucking crazy, completely unpredictable, and without a care for this life. They have nothing on you.

But you don't act. You offer a forearm, which João grips, and you lift him up and over the gunnel. He doesn't weigh a lot. He's always been a trim man, disciplined, self-controlled. The man you once hoped to become. *Now is the time to act, if you're going to, now's the time to take these guys out, one shot each, like they do in the movies,* but you don't, you just watch Salazar straddle the gunnel; then, incredibly, he's standing next to João, smiling at you under his black knit cap, nodding amiably at Kelly and, craning around, at Mendoza. A fucking meet-and-greet. Let's break the ice, get to know each other. Salazar seems like such a nice man, maybe 50, a little older than you, with a touch of gray in his closely cut hair.

"Welcome aboard," you tell them. Then: "What the hell am I saying? The *Padre Pio* belongs to João."

"Yes, it does," says João, straining not to say something more, the scaffolding of his musculature trembling, you can see now, as though he's trying to make a good impression, which is usually superfluous, because everyone likes João; there's never been any choice in the matter. He's João.

"Kelly," he says, "how was the trip out?"

"Oh, João, you know." Kelly leans forward awkwardly to take João's hand. "How're you holding up?"

João turns to offer Mendoza his hand as well. Mendoza takes it, limply. "Sorry about all this," says João. "It's not my choice."

"Actually, João, we're a little low on fuel," says Kelly,

his voice modulating now, as if in genuine deference to a superior. "We're running on fumes, and if you're looking for someone to blame—" He jerks a thumb at you. "Look no further than this man. But then you know how he is—better than anyone."

"Anyway, we're here," you say. Feeling the pistol in your hand, you run your thumb over the Portuguese coat of arms one last time, turn and offer it up to João handle first. Looking down at it, he seems a little dazed. "This is yours, too."

João glances at Salazar, who hasn't stopped smiling. He shrugs, as though a little embarrassed, tilts his head, and crosses his arms. João won't take the gun.

"No, no, that was a gift," he says, as though embarrassed himself. "You hold onto it."

You search his eyes, savor his expression, believe you detect a tremor, an incremental declination of the head, a matter of millimeters this way and that. Then, it's unmistakable: his eyes dart to his left. At one of the other men, come up for a look-see of his own. He's balancing at the top of the rope ladder, not yet officially aboard, one hand steadying himself on the rusted gunnel, the other trying to keep his shotgun trained on Mendoza.

"Anyway," João says, suddenly bright, "that's not what we're here for, is it?"

"Right." You part your jacket, slide the ledger free of your waist band, hold it aloft. "This is."

João squints, grows deathly serious, nods. Behind him, Salazar is bouncing slightly on the balls of his feet.

His head level, his eyes are all over the place, mostly on the man at the gunnel.

You're thinking, *Is it now? Am I already dead?* Mendoza is pressing into you with his eyes, furious and miserable, and you want to tell him to stop thinking, just stop with the mental calculations. What the fuck does he expect from you? He's standing there with a full banana clip; the man has a voice in all this. And he could end it all in a flash. Bring the whole fucking road show to its absurd conclusion.

"Well," says Kelly, awkwardly, "there you have it."

"There it is," you say, still holding the ledger out. You raise the pistol to scratch behind your ear, an involuntary move. Suddenly alert, Salazar uncrosses his arms and you see that his holster is empty, that, miraculously, he's holding his sidearm. That it's cocked. It's pointed at you, the dot of blackness that's the muzzle like a period. You're thinking, *Go for the man at the gunnel first.* You finally meet Mendoza's eyes. You feel the rosaries at your neck, beneath your shirt, burning your flesh, and you're tempted to start into another *Hail Mary.* The idea comes to you singed with nostalgia.

But you don't pray. You open fire.

Because it's all so effortless, you wonder what you could be doing wrong. So seamless and easy, it's really no big deal at all. Who needs to aim? *Aiming's for pussies!* One round in the general direction of the man at the gunnel, it misses him, OK, but the fucker reels, his arms slicing the damp air, then falls back just the same, though not before discharging the shotgun at Mendoza, the muzzle flaring red and yellow and your ears set to ringing, and there follows a series of sounds that can't be right, not in their apparent sequence, but then time is a damp stack of tissue, not a clean hard line, and you hear the complicated crunch of the gunnel man hitting the deck of the outboard 15 feet below *before* you see the flash of Salazar's pistol as he fires past João's ear *at you*, the fucker. *At you!* But no matter because he's already coming apart at the shoulder, in an embarrassing burst of personal moisture that leaves a João-shaped silhouette of dryness *on you*. And it has to be the easiest thing in the world: to keep your feet just where they are or else you won't see Kelly lurching backward toward the drag chains, gargling bubble noises, his hands at his throat. As Salazar lunges right, throws a leg over the gunnel, you're thinking, *you fucker, what do you know? There it is: so easy when you don't duck. That's the secret. You just keep shooting.* Behind you, Kelly's ugly gargling has shaded into of a moist wail, embarrassing, intimate. *Simple: don't look at him.* Salazar tumbles over the gunnel, brazenly, the man is actually attempting to climb down without a substantial portion of his shoulder. You hear João, some- where, say, "Don't." Then: "Let him go." So it's up for grabs as to exactly what the captain of the ship is ordering you to do as Salazar falls the last ten feet to the deck of the outboard. You don't see it happen, but you hear him hit through the ringing, feel it maybe, bone on unyielding aluminum and fiberglass. He's wailing too—*so much pain in this world*, as you fight the urge to laugh out loud at your appalling insensitivity—and he's doing it, the wailing, in Spanish or Portuguese. Screeching, actually. You glance over at João—he's hunched down between his bony shoulders—then you crouch with him at the gunnel as round after round flits up along the hull of the *Padre Pio*, from just below you, tracing a series of rude bright bee lines out above your head. You want to look over the side; something tells you not to. It might be João's voice. But another voice is saying: *follow through, candy ass, don't forget how easy it is—and you love it, don't you—just don't duck, because that's it, ducking is the mistake they all make. Not you. You're different.*

You rise to peer over the gunnel, João's hand slick on your wrist, offering resistance, as the third man in the boat keeps up the wide swings of his weapon, spraying the hull of the *Padre Pio*, the rounds singing past you, singing and tumbling harmlessly into the void. You smile. You aim, fire, and take off the upper third of the man's head. Easy. He falls back in the bow. Absolutely nothing to it.

Salazar bleeds and lumbers and stumbles over the gear to the stern—to what? set up clumsily behind the wheel? Fine. You ease the pistol over, it's already aimed, and squeeze off two rounds, not too smooth, the second recoil almost hitting you in the nose as Salazar jams the throttle in reverse, the back-momentum jolting him into the controls, and the boat jets into the first arc of a spiral, banking right sharply, the mosquito whine of the engines coiling up and out into space and away from the *Padre Pio*. With each pass, you watch as Salazar's body slumps more profoundly to the deck, one man in the water already, but Salazar and the other guy, who thanks to you isn't moving on his own anymore, are nudged centripetally toward the stern. It isn't long—how long, you can't tell—before Salazar's up and over the tilted gunnel himself, his neck and shoulder wallowing in the outboard's frothy wake. "Look," you yell, squeezing João's hand. On the very next pass, the aluminum bow cracks Salazar once in the skull, the props catch him with a tearing sound that momentarily raises the pitch of the whine. *That's that, is it?* The boat spiraling away with a dead man in the bow. He's not going anywhere. That's that.

João is urging you to the deck, whispering, "Easy."

"You see how I handled that?"

"Easy."

Over the receding whine of the outboard engines, something in you takes note of how much the reeling world has settled into shocking calm. To the north, Mendoza lies with his right knee up and tilted against the gunnel. South of you, Kelly lies arched backward over tangles of drag chains and steel-belted dampers, one loafer in the air, the other flung off somewhere. His basketball socks are filthy. But at least he's stopped gargling and grinding his teeth. That he's no longer moving, though, is just as annoying.

"Hey, Kelly," you yell, "stop fucking around."

"No." João tries to quiet you. "No more."

"Then make him stop," you say. "You can do that."

Beyond João's head, gulls trace and retrace their lines against a nacreous glow. The coming daylight. Mother of Pearl.

"Kelly," you yell, your eyes closed, "you think that's

fucking funny?" You call to Mendoza, "You see this guy? This asshole?" then struggle to rise on your elbows for a better view. But it pains you beyond words to put any weight on your elbows, your chest and shoulder blade and everything between having been wired for electricity and seemingly doused with warm diesel. Tight and ready to blaze. Still, you manage long enough to see the pulpy litter of hair and the white nodules and the aerosol of grit against the rust of the far gunnel. Yes, you decide, it's quite serious. Then you're furious. "Be that way!"

"Quiet now," says João. The sun has crested the horizon. The shadow of the gunnel rises and falls against his face. Where has the time gone?

"How's Mendoza?" you ask him. It's a test.

He smooths his damp, rough palm across your forehead. "He's OK." You don't like the look on his face. That disapproval or disappointment, that burnt expression, like all those times you argued over chess. Maybe it's just sadness. Just the way he's always been.

"Don't lie to me, João." You struggle with the rosaries around your neck. When he realizes what you're doing he finds your hand and lays them in it. You finger each bead, one to the next, searching. They seem huge. But you can't find the Y, you can't find the junction, just decade after decade. "Shit, João."

"Not that," he says, squeezing your fist around them. "The language, not now." His voice seems of a piece with your new physical knowing, which surges forward beyond description: a hollowness edged by pain. Tender as a wound. What worries you most, though, is your suspicion that it's always been there, this hollowness: the pain is what shows you where it is, otherwise how would you know? There's nothing else to rim the emptiness.

João's kind face against the sky makes you forget this foolishness. When he makes the sign of the cross, his fingers are damp with your blood, and they leave some of you behind on his forehead, his eyes shining wet. *Don't do that*, you want to say. *Don't cry.* But you won't embarrass him. You won't insult his dignity. That's what you tell yourself, comforting and pathetic, knowing full well that you can't speak even if you try. You close your eyes for a moment, you feel him shaking you awake, you open them again. But everything is growing stiff and useless. Everything is seizing up. Shutting down. Wave upon wave of fatigue and sound: they lift and lower your uselessness, and with each crest and trough, you cede that much more of what it takes just to pull the air into your lungs to speak. It should happen of its own, you want to tell João, you shouldn't have to think about breathing.

From the pilot house, a voice is calling out in the familiar squelchy tonalities of high-frequency radio communications. Beyond the gunnel, the outboard continues to recede, from the sound of it, whining as it orbits in reverse around an imaginary point, the point itself adrift. You're thinking of three words that you refuse to say. Why? Is it still about you?

From the radio in the pilot house, that voice again: "Duchand! Can you hear me? A Dios, my friend! To God! Duchand!"

Then you realize that all this time the *Padre Pio* itself

has been drifting, eastward, toward an equally imaginary point on the horizon.

The wind is whistling in the outriggers.

ACKNOWLEDGMENTS

I *WOULD LIKE TO THANK* the following people and organizations for their support and encouragement during **Night Work**'s long journey into the light: Mark Powell; Ron Phillips; Nicki Duval; my mother, sister, and brother; Leslie Daniels; and The Collegeville Institute.

My deepest gratitude goes to Ashley Alliano, my North Star.

PETE DUVAL is the author of two award-winning collections of short fiction: ***Rear View*** (Mariner, 2004), which won the Bakeless Prize, the Connecticut Book Award, and was a finalist for a Los Angeles Times book award; and ***The Deposition*** (University of Massachusetts Press, 2021) winner of the 2020 Juniper Prize for Fiction. The recipient of fellowships from Bread Loaf and the Collegeville Institute, Pete teaches at West Chester University in Pennsylvania and lives in Jersey City, NJ, with his wife and daughter, and four cats.

ABOUT
SHOTGUN HONEY BOOKS

Thank you for reading **Night Work** by Pete Duval.

Shotgun Honey began as a crime genre flash fiction webzine in 2011 created as a venue for new and established writers to experiment in the confines of a mere 700 words. More than a decade later, Shotgun Honey still challenges writers with that storytelling task, but also provides opportunities to expand beyond through our book imprint and has since published anthologies, collections, novellas and novels by new and emerging authors.

We hope you have enjoyed this book. That you will share your experience, review and rate this title positively on your favorite book review sites and with your social media family and friends.

Visit ShotgunHoneyBooks.com

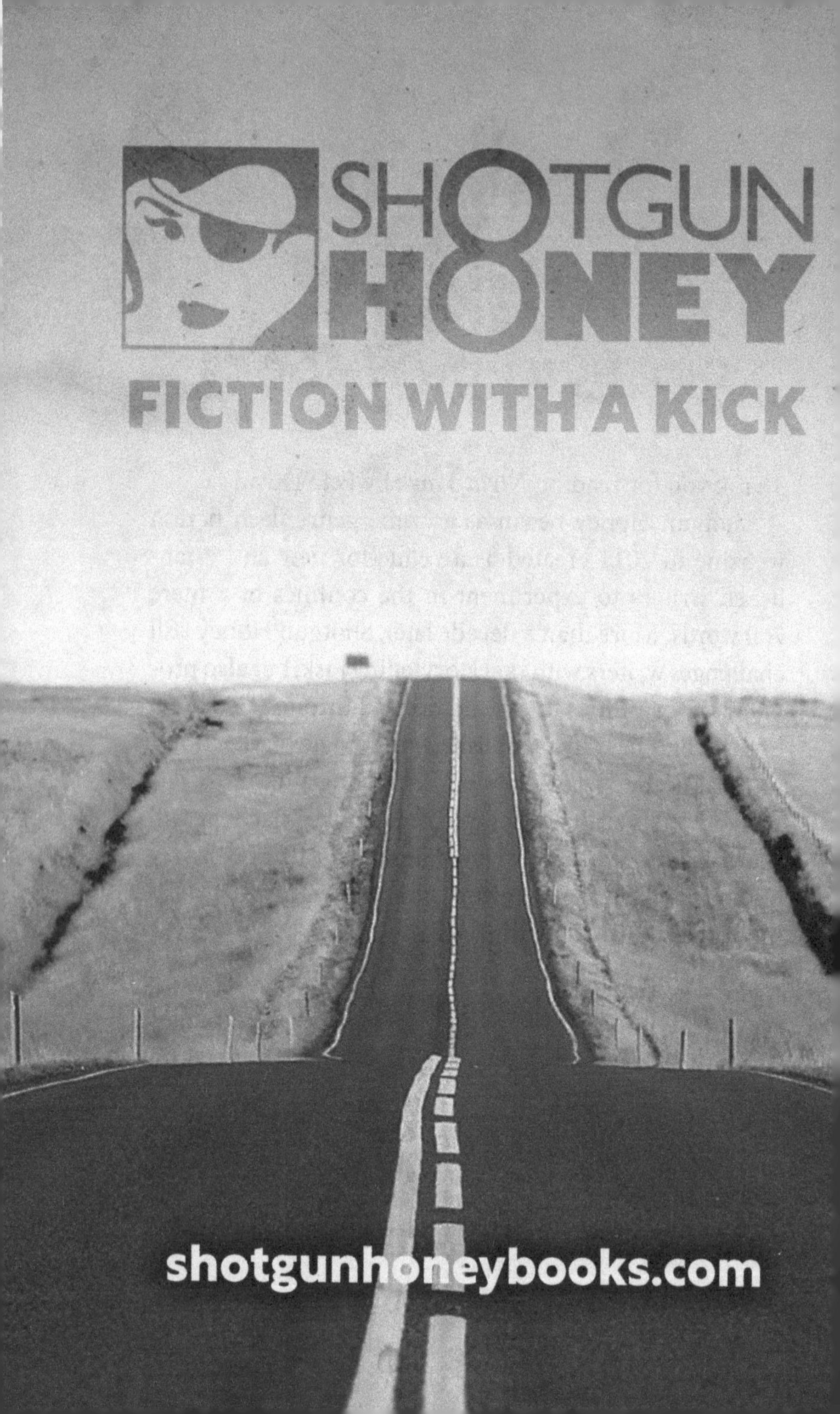

shotgunhoneybooks.com

www.ingramcontent.com/pod-product-compliance
Lightning Source LLC
Chambersburg PA
CBHW011807200726

48289CB00016B/3104